Fresh Burnt Laundry

By

Timothy Allen Smith

ISBN-978-1-960853-33-2

Liberation's Publishing LLC
Columbus - Mississippi

This book is for us. It's up to you to decide who "us" is and whether you're a part of it.

Table of Contents

1 F#ck My Life!

Light. It's blinding, fluorescent, every god damn where piercing through my eyelids and awaking me from a slumber close of that of a hibernating bear because of the fucking a/c that never cuts off. I open my eyes and stare at a ceiling that has more four-foot fluorescent light bulbs than stars in the sky. The guy four feet away from me lets out one of those five in the morning farts that feels great, but when heard nauseates the hearer. I think to myself, "Fuck my life!"

This is a human warehouse, the penal system in America. At this particular spot we have good food, satellite tv, marijuana, and cell phones, along with fifty men, four toilets, four showers, synthetic marijuana, crystal meth on occasion, and deplorable living conditions. There are a few good men, a slew of "grown men" with the minds of adolescents, good guards, bad guards, and pretty much anything else you can imagine. This room "our zone" in essence is a world within the world, and it's all we got. It contains everything else that the outside world contains but in a condensed and usually more intense form. We have love, hate, peace, war, lover's quarrels, religion, laughing, crying, joy, sadness and we have each other. Yet, we are all alone. This is our life.

By now, the air conditioner has blown the remnants of the beans my neighbor ate for lunch yesterday over to my rack, and I decided that's my cue to get up, brush my teeth, make some coffee, and wait on the six-a.m. count. This is my twelfth jail or prison throughout my criminal career, so I'm pretty well versed in how it all goes. What is the old saying? "Once you've seen one you've seen them all." Something like that. Either way that saying applies. So, teeth are now brushed, coffee is heating in the microwave. Since I'm the only one up I look at all twenty-five bunk beds filled with forty-nine men, and think to myself, "Fuck my life!"

Ding! The coffee is done, and I snap out of it, ease back to my rack, sit down, roll up a cigarette, enjoy it and my coffee and realize, "it ain't all that bad." I think to myself, how simple creatures we really are. How a cup of freeze-dried coffee and the cheapest cigarette tobacco in the world can bring a man in my situation joy baffles me, but it does. Here I am sitting and enjoying them both.

Six o'clock in the morning hits and here, right on time, come two correctional officers with clipboards in hand to count their sheep. They walk through flipping up towels and sheets that guys have wrapped around their bunks. Essentially, they've made tents out of the bottom bunks which prevent tanning from the fluorescent light, provide quite the lover's retreat for those who swing that way, allows use of cellphones while obstructing "Uncle's" view through his ever-watching camera system. It also gives us a good old war of wits to wage with the CO's. They take em down and we put em back up. It may seem trivial to you, but in the grand scheme of things you really can't give an inch. Once lost, some things can't be gained again. It's really about freedom, which in this world is only an idea, far from a reality. Whether or not we've ever been free I'll never know. I do know that we are far from it now. I don't just speak of those of us incarcerated. I'm talking about you as well.

You're free to drive as long as you follow all rules, have insurance, a tag, don't sing while driving, keep it under fifty-five, never make eye contact with a passerby, all your lights work, there are no cracks in your windshield, you've got fourteen inches of ground clearance between bumper and pavement, your exhaust isn't too loud, your truck isn't' too high, your window tint isn't too dark, you keep your radio turned down to a certain level and your vehicle meets all CPA regulations. Damn near damned if you do and damned if you don't. No wonder I'm locked in the freest most law having country in the world. Hence, we don't give an inch in here. We don't have an inch to give. It won't be long before those of you out there realize the same thing.

The CO's finish their count, it clears, and a couple more of the ruffians are up and about. Some were washing faces and brushing teeth while others were chasing the high in which they prefer. The door swings open again, and the feeding call is sounded, "Trays!" "Sleep late lose weight!", "Chow going back!", "Mainline!", or whatever different combo of words all meaning the same thing, time to eat. Most everyone is up and in line to receive a glorious breakfast of oatmeal and whatever else our patrons, the great taxpayers of America, provide us with this blessed morning. We eat and then comes the customary shit talking of those who didn't get their tray and those who grabbed the extra one. Every once in a while, we will have a fight over this issue. It's another one of those never-ending battles. While enjoying my oatmeal the thought of puppies fighting over the tit comes to mind, and I enjoy a good laugh with myself. In the right environment, mankind truly isn't much above the other beast of the earth.

Five minutes later things are settled down, bellies are full, and most are back in bed to sleep until lunch time. The hard life of a convict. I had a celly one time who said, "You know they wash our clothes, give us food, pay the cable bill, and pretty much do what we ask. It may take a month or two, but we've got it made bro." I wasn't quite sure what to say about that, but his words never left me. So here I sit listening to snoring and the morning news. Snoring is far better for the mind of a thinker, so I insert my ear plugs kick back and do some thinking.

"My name is Time! My name is Tiiiiiimmmmmmee!" is all I hear over and over as I'm awakened out of the nap that I slipped into after getting lost in my thoughts. A quick glance around and I know exactly what is going on. Someone "done" smoked too much of the spice. Spice is sprayed on paper and smuggled in through the mail in letters, birthday cards, or pictures. Some say it's nothing more than a couple of good coats of roach and wasp spray on paper. They cut it into little squares, and these guys smoke the fuck out of it. They love it. The downside is what's happening today with the fellow behind me. Some have occasionally died and even more have slipped into an alternate reality like this one has apparently done.

He is tripping balls. Some are laughing, some are pissed off, some are paranoid, and others are nonchalant about the situation. None of us want the police down here because this fuckhead has done smoked some shit that he can't handle. Now he thinks he is Father Time incarnate. The dumb motherfucker has already woken half of us up. If the police come down here and shake us down behind his bull shit, I risk losing my extra blanket, (which is grounds for a good beating). Some risk losing their cell phones, (which is grounds for a killing). Others risk losing any other type of contraband they may have, (which is also grounds for death).

So now everyone is in "get this bastard under control mode." Some are trying to get him on his bunk. Others are dashing him with cold water. The rest are hiding shit wherever they know how to hide it. Shit just got real that fast! Five minutes later, it's all over and the guy knows his real name again. He can't remember a single thing that happened. He is soaking wet, has a migraine, and just threw up his continental breakfast. The cops didn't come and that put everyone at ease and gave a good laugh at Father Time's expense.

Time passes and the door swings open and the feeding call is sounded. Like clockwork, breakfast and lunch, every day, is announced this way with minor changes in the faces, food, and festivities. Maybe life ain't so bad on the inside. Then again maybe it is, but we're all just so fucked up we can't tell the difference. It's Thursday so that means chicken. Let me tell you "wall street" hustlers ain't got shit on a prison chow table on chicken day. Guys have sold chicken three weeks in advance for everything from cigarettes to drugs. We've got deals ranging from green beans for cornbread, juice packet for cake, chicken for hamburger tray, two shots of coffee for a soul and anything else that can be bartered is bartered. Everything is worth something here. Aint' shit free.

The most notorious trade of all is the old icy white honey bun on your pillow trade. If you eat it, the man who put it there is going to want the exact same one back. Yeah, shit just got real. He may even use the classic line of, "shit on my dick or blood on my shank" when he comes for that honey bun. I recommend eating the honey bun but be prepared to knock the faggot out when he comes for it back. Free honey bun and rec all at the same time.

Lunch passes without an incident like it does more often than not and it's time to crank up the spades, dominoes, and chess games. Most don't go back to sleep after lunch, so the zone is a modge-podge of activity. This is when you hear all of the shit that happens behind closed doors. My first time through I almost lost all hope in humanity. I was saddened to hear what I heard and see what I saw. Men can be despicable creatures. Just as a coin has two sides so do men. I've thought to myself after meeting a few individuals that there was no good in man only for God to prove my thoughts wrong in the future. The same individual I thought was unredeemable and I crossed paths with again just so that I could see the good in them that I thought wasn't there.

"Let the card games begin!" I'm playing with my usual crew, which is made up of three rascals who cheat, lie, and love talking shit. I don't gamble so I've nothing to lose from cheating. Lies stopped bothering me when I found out Santa was bullshit. So, when there's nothing better to do, may as well talk shit!

First diamond gets the deal, and it falls to the man across from me. He is approaching sixty years old, with long hair in a ponytail, no tattoos, which is rare, and shifty eyes. He ain't never crossed me though so I could care less what he's done or does as far as that goes. Spades is the game, so he and I are partners since we're sitting across from one another. He deals out our thirteen cards and I've got one book. Luckily, the first hand is open, and we only need four books. Which is what we get nine to four their way to start the game. The man to my right begins shuffling the cards and my partner is turned around watching a commercial on the television. It goes off and he says, "well that's good news right there, boys. You can now pound the prostate of another man. As long as you take that pill you won't catch the HIV from the queer." I have no words, but we all erupt into laughter. You can't make this shit up and win, lose or draw that comment made the game worth playing.

We go on to lose thirty-five to thirty-one in our first game of spades. My partner and I won the next game and I need a break. My ass has done started hurting from sitting on this bullshit steel picnic table and I need a smoke and cup of coffee. Both of which are sometimes more valuable than gold inside this concrete jungle. Don't' get it fucked up. This is the concrete jungle. It's dangerous, easy to get into, hard to get out of, and slam filled with animals. Luckily, we adapt quickly to our environment.

I just sit here, smoke my cigarette, sip my coffee, and enjoy the show. My neighbors are arguing about who has more money, Jay-Z or Kanye West. I'm not really sure what it really matters in the grand scheme of things, but these two must really care. I've heard that exact same conversations somewhere between one-hundred-sixty-three, and two-hundred and twelve times. I get the numbers mixed up but between that one and who is the better basketball player, Michael Jordan or Lebron James. Both conversations can become very heated and are obviously sincerely held beliefs and also the dividing line amongst many of the dark-skinned comrades of mine here in the jungle. If they were only talking of taxes and law and the government instead of that bullshit, we may be able to make a difference in the world, but here we are and there they go again. Groundhog's Day!

Don't think they are alone in the bullshit. My own people seem to be worried more about getting high, and what this or that bitch's ass looks like. I like a nice ass and getting high as well, but god damn they aren't number one or number two on my list of shit I give a fuck about. I guess life really is all about priorities. Our situation seems hopeless at times. But when has the world ever been what it could be?

Thinking makes me hungry so it's time for that penitentiary staple the "Ramen Motherfuckin Noodle!" I prefer a chili with a pack of hot sauce flavored pork skins and occasionally a mackerel pack thrown in as well. I'll never forget the first time I smelt that combination cooking in the microwave. It smells like something you wouldn't want to put your finger or pecker in and definitely wasn't something you'd want to eat. Boy how things have changed. This meal now makes my stomach growl. It still doesn't smell like something I want to stick anything in though. Maybe I'm becoming a savage or maybe I'm just hungry or maybe I'm fucked up. Hell! Who knows or better yet who gives a fuck.

I prepare my meal and get to thinking about my situation. On the outside looking in it would seem bleak, but I'm not guilty of two of the charges they've got on me. I know one thing about the law, system, and people who are part of it, they can do whatever in the fuck they want to do. The real world ain't nothing like those bullshit tv shows. Lady justice is blind in one eye and can't see out the other. So, if you ever find yourself in this type of situation admit your guilt, kill the truth, say you're sorry, and ask for mercy.

It's better not to say anything before you lie. Lies are an insult to people's intelligence and aren't respected. So, you are better off remaining silent than telling a lie. All fifty of us in here are pre-trial. Most refuse to face reality and damn sure don't want any advice. I've seen guys think they were going home on probation come back from court with thirty years with tears streaming down their face. Good guys get ten years, and the worst of the worst get two. The shortfall of our justice system. If you ever get caught up in it, do all you can, while trying to retain your honor, to get out. The key is to prove you aren't just what you did.

I believe I've done that. Even though an evil bitch filed false police reports, lied, stole, and tried her damnedest to have me thrown away to never see the light of day again, there is a just God who knows when one of his own has been wronged. Even though man's law doesn't line up with God's law he can still work miracles to affect the outcome of one's punishment. Just as King David, so do I rely on the Lord for protection. As long as I don't do what I know in my heart to be wrong, me and the Almighty are on good terms. Hence, they try to get rid of me, but the Lord thwarts their plans and here I sit with some good, some bad, some happy and some sad men. Men we are and in God we believe. Justice, we doubt, and the capabilities of men we know.

Of the laws I did break I'll be sentenced to a couple years in prison while the person who broke one of God's ten commandments and completely falsified a story about a felonious crime, gets cursed out and sent on her way. That's the justice of the world and that is why I trust in God and not men. That's enough of that line of thought. I have to leave vengeance up to the Lord. If not, with all this time, I would plan a way for her to destroy herself and sit back and play the hand of providence. I mean, would it be wrong to arrange a chocolate cake to tempt a diabetic with a label that says, "sugar free" even though it's packed full of sugar? You see anyone can be got with enough planning. The goal is to have them destroy themselves by their own vices. Therefore, know their weakness and you are their master. I will wait for God to do his job and hopefully be able to keep the blood off my hands and conscience.

All of a sudden, "Get against the fuckin wall!" is shouted while ten correction officers run in for a shake down. Shake down is what we call searches where the CO's come in ransacking everything, strip search us, take all the contraband they can find with the intent of selling it back to us for a nice little profit. Shaking my balls at another man used to be embarrassing, but over time it's become just another day at the office. I even had "Your Favorite Part" tattooed below my belt line to lighten the mood, like to ask them if this is their favorite part of the job.

So, we are now headed into the showers four at a time, told to drop'em, squat and cough, which we all do. The guard who was searching me takes a double take at my tattoo but that's about the only reaction. If my dick were bigger, he might have laughed at the smiley face smoking a joint on the head of it, but he probably didn't notice it from that distance. Nothing fell out of my asshole when I squatted and coughed so I'm herded off to the front of the zone with the other black sheep of the world to wait on the COs to finish searching.

By the time it's all said and done we've lost two men. One had his cellphone hid in his mat and they found it, the other had a shank in a pair of shoes under his rack. Neither will be missed as they were both loudmouth dumbasses. The zone isn't any worse we are down a couple cell phones some homemade knives and two that we will be fine without. I didn't personally lose anything, so I remade my bed, straightened out my locker box, and sat down to listen to the nonsense. As always people are accusing others of snitching. They are like vultures on the property of the two who are headed to the hole and laughing about all the shit they didn't find. It's the same shit every time.

Thirty-minutes later and it's dinner time. Cornbread, cake, beans, and rice with mystery meat. Not too sure about the rest of the country, but here in Mississippi you can bet on cornbread with at least two meals a day and you god damn right I'm eating my cornbread. That's dinner and all that's left to look forward to today. Fuck my life!

I decided it was time to move around a little, so I started walking circles around the zone. This is where you learn to use your peripheral vision. You walk and see without looking. You listen without repeating and round and round you go like a fucking hamster in a wheel. Always going but never getting anywhere. Never felt sorry for the furry little bastards until I was put in the same predicament. I guess that goes without saying I would never own a hamster, but here I walk around and around and here I think about what's up and down.

I figured out on my first five-year bid that "Once you've stopped worrying about whether or not your kids will forget you and the things that are out of your control, your mind will be left open to higher things. Some guys build relationships to network when they get out, some learn new hustles, some find God, and some very few use this time to see the world for what it really is. When everything is provided to you and your only concern is staying alive you can elevate. This is not what they want, believe me. What they want is for you to believe the news, think politicians are needed, laws don't impose on freedom and that you're supposed to work for forty years or more to retire before age renders you disabled and you live off the crumbs you're given while those in power rape, rob and pillage your country for everything it's worth. They want you to vote left or right and they want you to know it's the lessor of two evils. You voted but somehow, they don't want you to realize that voting for the lesser of two evils is voting for evil. Fuck my life!

I used to think I was crazy for thinking shit like that but thanks again to the penal system in America. I've been evaluated by several psychologist along the way and they all seem to think I'm just fine. Even told one about a quarrel that I had with God. How when I told the Creator to show up if it was his hand that caused a certain situation so he and I could settle the dispute. A being in the same image of a man but made of light particles the colors of lapis lazuli showed up. I didn't think the Glock I held in one hand or the AR-15 in the other were the correct weapons for that battle so I didn't fire. The shrink looked at me and said, "You're not crazy, just sounds like God is working in your life." I knew then it wasn't me but the rest of the world that was fucking nuts!

I stopped by one of the card tables before my mind took my feet off the ground and watched the guys play a couple of hands. I see one of them throw a heart when spades were the suit played even though he has a spade in his hand. Obviously, he is cheating but it's not by business to say anything. This is a case when the "hear no evil, speak no evil and see no evil" law applies. I continue to watch and two books later the player who used a heart and saved his spade plays the spade and the table erupts in an argument. This is my cue to get back to walking and that's what I do.

The next lap around I pass the guys playing cards and they are still arguing. Luckily, they aren't gambling for any noodles, or the situation would've undoubtedly turned into a fight already. One of the guys tries dragging me into the situation but I just smile and keep on keeping on. I may break the law, but I'm no fool. I only break laws I believe are bullshit anyways, but I don't feel like getting into that right now. So, I walk, and I look, and I listen, and I think. I think about how eighty-seven out of one hundred of us will come back to prison after this bid. I think about how the government tells all the rest of you that they try to help us while we are here. I think about how ya'll believe it. I think about good men who make a mistake and then turn bad just to survive in here. I think for those around me who aren't too good at thinking for themselves and then I think about what I can do to help us all out. And then I think, I'm done thinking for the day.

Everyone running up to the front of the zone brings me back to reality and all its flaws. The nurse is doing her nightly rounds, and the animals are all quaking and lusting over something they can't have. This is truly a disheartening sight but nevertheless it goes on every day in every facility. She picks up the sick calls from the drop box and passes out a few medications and is forced to turn around and leave. These motherfuckers are like rabid dogs that smell a female in heat on the other side of a fence. I've no doubt that if I had a pineapple grenade, I'd pull the pin and gently roll it into the crowd of animals who are standing up front grabbing their dicks and talking about this woman like they don't have a mother, sister, daughter, or manners as far as that goes. Definitely wish I had a grenade.

You know, some people truly belong here. There is evil in the world but a lot of guys behind these bars and fences don't feel like they've done wrong. We all know we were breaking the law, but not so many of us feel like we are wrong for it. I mean we live in a county in which everyone is a lawbreaker at some point, so why should we feel wrong as long as we didn't hurt anyone who didn't deserve it?

This will give you an idea of how fucked up a country we live in. I, a convict, have had conversations with law enforcement officers about what they are to do when faced with a situation in which they must enforce the law or do what their hearts tell them is right. This shouldn't be, the two should align. A man should never be forced to choose between his job or doing what is right, but whether you know it or believe it this is going on every single fucking day, and I for one am sick of it.

Next, they bring in a laundry cart. It's nearly nine o'clock at night by now, but that means nothing here. Everyone puts their laundry in the laundry bag and throws it in the cart. They'll be back sometime tomorrow. A couple of guys have bedded down for the night, but the rest of the zone is carrying on like it's nine o'clock in the morning. Ain't no rest for the wicked I reckon.

Night shift is always more understaffed and more chill than day shift which is why guys are up right now. The cellphones come out of where they've been hiding. The wood gets fired up as well as the spice and meth. I mean looking around right now the only thing that's missing is women, which is not to say we don't have the next best thing.

A dude wearing the laundry bag sewed into a skirt if you swing that way. Hell, it's a regular shin dig in here. And it ain't even the weekend.

So, I kicked back and enjoyed the show. Me, I like to get a high, but there's a time and place for everything, and this isn't the time or the place for me to be doing that. To each his own. From looking around I can tell this is the perfect time and place for some others who don't know this rule, and this is the wrong time and place for them, but they do it anyway. The fucking correctional officers must sit in the towers and trip out at the shit they see and hear. I'm smack dab in the middle of it and ain't never seen a tv show more entertaining than this shit.

I drift off to sleep only to be awakened suddenly by another spice episode, god damn closet smokers who are too ashamed and afraid to smoke the paper covered with roach spray or whatever chemical it's covered with, wait until the middle of the night to smoke this shit, and then wake the whole unit up when they start tripin. This guy is on his knees in the bathroom with tears in his eyes saying, "Please, Jesus, talk to him for me, I don't want Daniel to take my soul to hell forever." A quick look around and I see this episode is a little more serious than the one earlier today. Maybe it's because it's the middle of the night. Either way everyone is aggravated. Then the police came in.

The man is still trying to strike a deal with Jesus, and the fucking COs don't know what to do. He is still on his knees crying. Half the people are laughing, some are praying, some are hiding contraband, and the cops don't know whether to tazze ole boy, mace his ass, handcuff him or call the fucking priest to perform an exorcism. This shit has got real. So, I light up a cigarette and lace up my shoes just in case. The police finally get the man who lost his soul to calm down enough to cuff him and take him on out of here. He is either going to the hospital or the hole. We may never know which. It's nighttime and this jail, just like every other across the country, is understaffed. So, we don't receive any repercussions behind that fool's drug overdose. If they end up taking him to the hospital, we will probably receive some type of group punishment because the jail receives bad publicity from that. I mean, how do we get drugs and contraband while behind bars? We ain't going to Walmart and buying the cell phones ourselves.

It's still the middle of the night and we don't get breakfast until six in the morning, so guys who have food are eating and guys who don't are hungry. If you've ever been hungry and couldn't do anything about it, you know the feeling but if not, you don't know the struggle. It's a hopelessness that changes a man. Some will give all to satisfy the hunger, and on the same token some will gain all to feed the destitute. So, I see a guy trading his chicken next week for a noodle when next week the same chicken would be worth four noodles. The market definitely changes here, and the rich get richer, while the poorer get poorer. Although I've never understood how one can get rich off zoom-zooms and wham-whams, some must obviously know some secret I've yet to figure out.

Then I see one of those small acts of kindness that redeems my faith in the human race. It's only a ramen noodle that's given, but its given and not traded, and it's done where no one knows except the giver, the receiver, and me. The giver just so happens to be one of the animals that can't control himself around the nurse. This makes me glad I didn't have that grenade earlier. The recipient is an old man who is charged with commercial burglary for breaking into a parts supplier yard and cranking their parts truck to keep warm. He'd been doing it all winter, but he slept a little too long one morning and was awoken by the city police. Needless to say, the vagrant didn't have anything to give except food from his tray in the future so out of the good that exists in the animal's heart he gave the old man some food.

In a room with no walls and forty-nine other people you see the best and the worst in your fellow creatures. I don't expect you to know and I can't blame you for believing what you see on tv and hear on the radio, but there comes a time in all our lives when we must stop using excuses. So, I hope you can tell the difference between the truth and a lie before this is all over with. It was and is my goal. That's enough of all that for now. It's late and tomorrow is Friday and the day I get sentenced for the first of two times for the same crime.

Once again, a god damn flood of fluorescent light cuts through my eyelids damaging my pupil. I open my eyes, hear the first fart of the day, and think to myself, "Fuck my life!" We about to find out once again just how crazy I am. I've got to go to the Federal courthouse to be judged by the righteous Federal Government and weighed on the scales of justice by the all-seeing lady justice and finally be punished for breaking laws and committing crimes in which I didn't harm a soul. Thank God there is a God who doesn't let these fools completely loose or the rest of you'd be fucked just like us or maybe you already are and just don't know it yet. Remember that as of right now, you think I'm bat shit crazy. We will see where you stand by the time all of this is over with.

They come count as always, then breakfast trays come as always and then I sit and wait. I'm not really nervous. The most they can give me today is thirteen to twenty-four months, which is what the Feds sentence you in, instead of using the usual term years. They like to say months. This doctrine has guys up there trying to add the years up on their fingers after the judge drops the gavel. But anyways it's my day again and I've got to get judged again. The whole charade is comical, besides the fact that they are about to give me precious time of my life in prison. But besides that, this is what I find funny. They try and force people to put their hand on a Bible or raise one hand and swear to tell the truth when in that very same Bible in the book of Matthew Chapter 5:34-34 Jesus instructs us not to swear or take oaths at all. Just simply say yes or no because anything more than that cometh of evil. So, if you can get any more hypocritical than that I'd like someone to tell me how. Then we have the fact that not one single person in the entire country is a law-abiding citizen. It depends on who you are, how much money you have, who you know and what you've done. It will all determine whether you will stand before the not really so almighty Department of Justice to be judged. Then we have the fact that what our society accepts as laws are so flawed that it's a joke to be regulated or controlled or even sentenced by them. Now don't get me wrong, some things are wrong and should be illegal but if it's not wrong why should it be against the law? Therein lies my quarrel with the whole system.

Just because one man's beliefs and his rise to power gave him the ability to use ink to write words on a piece of paper does not mean that we should be forced to live our lives dictated by them. Do you still believe you are free? How do words on paper determine what's right or wrong? Shouldn't we have the freedom to decide that ourselves and shouldn't our hearts tell us what's right and what's wrong? I can't tell you what your preacher probably never told you. If you're a Christian anyways, Romans 2:3-16 basically says that we Gentiles demonstrate that God's law is written in our hearts by our actions, and that our own thoughts and consciences, either accuse or excuse us, and if your mind and heart say it's ok, and you are a follower of Christ's teachings, you are free to do what you believe is right. If you do wrong, you bring judgement on yourself from God and not some Mickey Mouse ass court who infringes on people's freedoms every single day while being so blind that they think they represent freedom.

So now you should be able to see part of the problem I have with our current situation. Of course, if you've never been through it, I wouldn't expect you to be conscious of it all. Honestly, even if you have, I can't expect that of you either. Sometimes we have inklings of things, but until someone puts into words what we feel, we aren't fully aware or completely conscious of what we are feeling, or why we feel something inside us isn't right. It just feels some kind of way. Now comes the flip side to the coin of knowing; once you know something you can't unknow it. Once you know something and do nothing you are accountable. Hence the old saying, damned if you do and damned if you don't.

So now I sit here and wait for someone to come and get me. It should be within the next hour, so I read over what I want to say before my sentence is passed down. I've got a couple points I want to make that way it's on the record. My thoughts drift to all the good men throughout history. What's sad is they were almost all martyred, kicked out of society, or called crazy. These men are my inspiration though. Men like Joseph who was falsely accused of rape, just as I was. He then rose to be second in all of Egypt and saved countless of thousands from famine. Think about Jesus who taught people the mystery of God one day and was hung on a cross the next for telling the truth. There were countless others who saw the evil in their government and ruling authorities and were killed, exiled thrown into prison, falsely accused, tortured, and killed all while never having harmed a soul. They were just merely speaking the truth and standing up for what was right against tyrants and the wicked rulers of the world. The masses believed what they were told. Their hearts were persuaded into hating what was good. They saw with their eyes instead of their mind. They understood with their ears instead of their heart. They could be influenced this way or that. I'm sickened at the thought of how after thousands of years people are still as simple and foolish as they were then. *Then they call my name and it's time I play my role in this never-ending story.*

Judgement time has come. I walk out of the unit, up to the booking area, going through the motions like a well-trained horse when it's time to be saddled. Raise right foot, guard puts on shackle. Raise left foot, on goes shackle. Hands up, on goes waist chain, turn around hands down, on goes handcuffs. The guard says, "I wish everyone would lift their feet that high, so I wouldn't have to bend down so damn far." I just smile and say, "I'm just a well-trained animal." He couldn't control the humanity that poured out of his eyes and we both walked to the sally port in silence.

A quick thirty-minute van ride, and we arrived at the Federal Courthouse downtown. As we walked up to the rear entrance, I noticed the thick granite panels that make up the exterior of the building. This shit is what people pay one hundred and fifty dollars a square foot for as countertops in their dream homes. Tens of millions of homeless people in America and our tax dollars get wasted on such as this. Once the guard enters the code in the keypad we enter, and I notice the granite walls on the interior as well. Fucking extravagant, no wonder we are trillions of dollars in debt. The dollar is so inflated it's almost cheaper to wipe your ass with a dollar bill than it is to buy good quality toilet paper, and the country is ready to erupt at the drop of a dime. Don't even get confused, the government is to blame for all of this.

So here I stand, family behind me, government henchmen and prosecutors to my left, my public pretender, I mean defender, on my right, and the honorable, holier than thou, stand when he enters, my chair is higher than yours, almighty judge in front of me. God I'm glad I'm not him. That may sound strange to you, but depending upon your beliefs, he may or may not be in a worse position than I am. Imagine being Pontius Pilate and being the man who sentenced the best man who walked the earth to death because that was his job. Now I hope you see my point of view. The judge must also know the scripture that says judge not and ye shall not be judged. His judgement will be coming from the judgement seat of God. So contrary to popular belief it can be worse.

All bullshit aside though some judges do stand for what's right. They probably feel like David in front of Goliath, or the way a little candle must feel, trying to light a dark room all by itself. They didn't write the laws and the laws are the problem. It does feel as if they are always on the side of the government when they should only be on the side of justice, but it is what it is for now.

So here I stand, and we go through the traditions of men before us. We rose when the honorable entered, then we sat. They called me up to the stage and tried to make me raise my hand and swear to tell the truth, which I politely refused. "Because off sincerely held religious beliefs your honor, I do not swear or take oaths, but I will affirm my word and plan on telling the truth." This ruffles their feathers a bit because most sheep do exactly as they are told, but I'm a human, not a sheep. So, I choose not to go along with the motions. "Sir you do understand that under the law of perjury that if you lie while on the stand, we can sentence you to five years behind bars?" The judge asked. I reply with a "Yes, Sir." then think to myself, "I may as well add that on to the other list of shit that I done." I then try to remember one time that I hurt someone. I can't think of one single crime that I committed against another person. Now I wonder if I'm really the bad guy or just someone who don't give a fuck about the law. Fuck my life!

So, the judge goes on to tell me that I was on probation and therefore not supposed to use, possess, or manufacture methamphetamine, all of which I am guilty of. I also wasn't supposed to have firearms, which I did. He goes on to tell me that I got to go to Federal Prison for eighteen months for the horrible, terrible crimes against humanity in which no one was injured or harmed. It was so covert that my neighbor nor my own mother knew what was going on. This is the judicial system in America.

"The gavel drops, I've been sentenced, and this is what all the fuss is about." So, that's eighteen months for violating my probation, and now I'll be transferred back into state custody to get sentenced on the same charges. Seems like two sentences for the same crime. Not according to them because the state and feds are two different "sovereigns" huh, so even if it is double jeopardy, it's ok as long as it's two different entities? This same scenario plays out every single day, in anything ranging from freedom of speech, if you don't threaten, harass, or terrify anyone or if you don't tell people the truth. It's played out with the right to bear and keep arms as long as they are a certain type of arms. They must register you must have never been convicted of a crime "whether against a person or not doesn't matter," and as long as you follow this long list of rules and regulations you can bear arms as defined in our constitution. George Washington, and the rest of the founding fathers would be ashamed of what they built has become. But at least they only gave me eighteen months instead of the high side of the guidelines which was twenty-one months. God, I hate Uncle Sam!

My family is five feet away from me, but I'm not permitted to hug them. It's been five months since I could touch my loved ones. These pretrial jails don't permit contact visits, so you either see your loved ones through glass or video chat. With them on a kiosk or tablet in the unit. Very humane, especially for a hardcore killer like me. I mean drug user and second amendment patriot. This mass incarceration should have struck close to your home by now. Get ready if it hasn't, but also try and see the person for who they are. The person you know because everyone has a vice and secret life. As long as they ain't hurting anyone they should be free to do as they please. That's the way it was meant to be anyways. So, I tell my folks bye, and am escorted out of the courtroom.

This scene brings back an old memory and the realization that all is not lost. Just as the US Marshall wouldn't let me see and hug my family there is always a flipside. Years ago, I was in a courthouse getting sentenced with family behind me. A sheriff, who actually treated people as people, unhandcuffed me and gave me a couple minutes in a private room with my family after sentencing. It's the small acts like that that restore faith in humanity and make me hope we can create a better world to live in.

So now we are headed back to the county jail. I know I won't be there much longer since I have been sentenced. I'll still have to go back to the neighborhood of my local county to be sentenced for still pending charges. The sentence I just received was my punishment for being on probation and catching new charges. I hope that makes sense to you because it seems like complete bullshit to me. But hey, I'm bat shit crazy and that's exactly how it goes down always. Remember kids, if the blind lead the blind we all fall into a ditch, break a hip, and receive disability and Medicaid for the rest of our lives. The machine that prints money will pay for it. Fuck my life!

Finally, back in the zone, I can relax. Hell, I'm so fucked up, the entire time that I was gone I just wanted to get back to the jail. No wonder I'm a repeat offender like 87 out of 100 other guys. But I'm back and I'm sitting on my rack trying to breathe after everyone bombarded me with questions about how much time I got. I'm not really sure how many of them are concerned. Whether they are sincere or nosey doesn't bother me. Hell, we are all in this shit together.

So here I sit knowing I've got an eighteen-month sentence to do after I finish this next sentence that I get. I let out a laugh. Fuck this country! Not the people or the land, but the establishment. Fuck it! And then I use my hatred as fuel, and I start thinking to myself, "How can one topple something so large, so strong, so dominating? Of course, it will take God to accomplish such a feat. How can I know God is on my side though? This is gonna take some soul searching and some question asking, and some answer finding." Seems like a daunting task, but it's one that I must take on. Or at least try and take it on. I guess we will see what happens.

Here I sit, and here I contemplate my situation, our world, our government, and my God. The situation is bleak, but light isn't too far around the corner. I already know my local county wants to give me two years for the meth manufacturing and firearms. The Feds gave me eighteen months, so that's three and a half years. I've got six months done already, so that leaves me three years to come up with a plan, make sure the Lord is on my side, and then build the army. The more I think about it the more feasible it all seems. The only dilemma I can see is making sure God is on our side. Lord knows we can't win if we oppose the Almighty! Hell, I suppose I'll just ask for a sign or an answer. So that's what I'll do, wait, and plan in the meantime.

My rack partner walks up and brings me back to reality with one of the dumbass questions he comes up with to create idle conversation. He is an alright guy, but doesn't fully comprehend body language and certain unwritten rules. For instance, if someone is reading a book or writing a letter, it's a pretty good indication that you should leave them the fuck alone, unless it's important or urgent news that you must tell them. Bless his poor little heart. He really just doesn't get it, and I don't feel like telling him he has the IQ of a chimpanzee. My eleven-year-old can carry on a more intelligent conversation than him. So, I don't. I tell him everything about the big field trip to court, and then it hits me. The smell that once has been smelt can never be un-smelt.

Fresh Burnt Laundry stings the nostrils, makes me feel all warm and fuzzy inside, and puts me in beast mode. I know there is a chance someone will accidentally, on purpose, steal my god damn laundry and force me to threaten, curse, and even talk shit about someone's mother until I get my shit back. It's a mad dash to the front of the unit and the laundry is thrown from a cart onto a table. We "look" like vultures on a dead animal as guys push, shove, knock shit on the floor, and finally run across the laundry bag with their name or gang sign written in it. Definitely not civilized and definitely no manners of concern for the next person either. If you're timid, you wait until the savages are out of the way, and hope there is still some meat on the bones or the laundry bag with your shit on it. I'm not timid, and I work my way to the front of the crowd. I see my boy across the table give me the "I got you," look, and then toss my laundry bag. It's still warm so I throw it over my shoulder. On the way back to my rack, I inhale the smell that is somehow bad and good at the same time. I look over and notice the coil spring a ½ inch from my cheek.

So, in case you didn't know, we have two types of springs that come back attached to your fresh burnt laundry. The coil spring and the leaf spring. Coil springs are tightly wound, jet black, and seem to be magnetic or magically clingy pubic hairs found on my brothers of another color from another mother "and father." Leaf springs tend to be long, with lazy loops, or sometimes just hills, and range from red, yellow, brown or black pubic hairs that come from my brothers of the same color but another mother "and father." These are less common as they don't tend to tangle themselves in other people's clothes quite as often as their counterparts. So now that you've been enlightened, I sit on my bunk and remove all pubic hairs from my fresh burnt laundry.

Time passes and it's lunch time. The exchange is open, and the trading has begun. We got cornbread for cake going once, and then twice, then the deal is made. Got a juice pack for two sugar packs off the next morning breakfast tray. Someone jumped on that shit quick. Then I hear, main course for a roll of toilet paper, which means somebody's ass is in a bind, and it goes quick. Man, the deals are jumping off today. So, I try my luck and see if anyone wants to sell me their soul for two mustard packs and a shot of coffee. I repeat it again, just a little louder this time. I get a couple of looks, but no takers. I think about throwing in a cigarette to sweeten the deal. I figure I may not be able to get my money back out of it at that price. So, I repeat my offer for the third and final time, but still don't get any bites. They all think I'm crazy already, so no one says anything. I get back to eating and they continue their day trading in peace. It was a good lunch.

Just like yesterday, and the day before we eat, we smoke, we talk shit, and then we play cards. I guess some watch tv, some play chess and some twiddle their thumbs. Whatever the case, it is just like playing cards, a big fucking waste of time and people. Don't get it twisted, there is evil in this world, and there are men who choose evil over good on a daily basis. They do belong here. But the irony is that most evil people in the world are usually praised, while the best men in the world are persecuted. This life is fucking insane.

So, I'm looking around at the forty-nine other gentleman in here, while trying to decide who is truly evil, and you know what I come up with? None of them! Believe it or not, I can't say any of these men are evil. They may have committed an evil act or some other horrendous crime, but after living with them all for six weeks or so now, my judgment is that none are consumed by evil. I've seen most of them do some fucked up shit. I've also seen the same ones redeem themselves by one kind act. Anyway, we sit here wasting away, and the thought hits me to start a conversation, or rather start the conversation. If conversation rules the nation, then the right conversation could also change the nation or perhaps even the world.

2 The Conversation

What would it be though? Who would it be amongst? Would anyone listen? Does anyone even care? I guess there's only one way to find out. My first thoughts are maybe I should include a ball or perhaps a frisbee. Does this sound crazy? Please let me elaborate. Just think about the passion people have for sports, hence ball. Since sports are basically people doing something with a ball, perhaps if I incorporate a ball into a movement, we could get people inspired. Or maybe I'm supposed to get their attention off of a ball long enough to realize they work roughly 8 out of 10 days for someone else's benefit. Then I think to myself "ball" god damnit! I even like balls. Ha! Not really, I'm beginning to despise them. It's sad that so many people care so much about something so foolish as a game played with a ball. This train of thought makes me wonder how God feels. Could you imagine people worshipping God with as they do while watching men in uniforms doing something with a ball? I bet the Lord would give you a sign if we were that loyal to the almighty.

No, I can't use a ball, because then people will only care about the ball, and we will be right back where we started. So, that means the trick to this will be making people care about something more than a ball. I light a cigarette and realize we may all be doomed. The fucked-up part is that sometimes I think I'm the only one aware of our situation. I guess that's how Atlas felt. Then, as I was woke from my slumber, I look thirteen feet in front of me and witness a man lying on his back with his knees up suddenly start fucking the air with hard upward pelvic thrusts. I mean, this fool is pounding that imaginary pussy. He is also talking to someone who either isn't there or is there and I just can't see her. I'll be damned if I know which one it is, either way I am entertained, amused, and appalled all at the same time. I guess this is the universe's way of making light of a heavy situation. So, here I sit, watching a crazy man fuck something that ain't there, and think to myself, it could be worse. Hell! I could be laying back in my rack having sex with some imaginary woman and I think to myself, "that fella has got it made." Suddenly, I envied him. I really must be losing my mind.

A friend walks up to enjoy the porn and share the laughter with me, and I ask him, "does anyone even care?" He quits laughing, looks at me with a quizzical, sideway glance and says, "about him?" as he pointed to the man who was still repeatedly dry humping the air. I shake my head and say, "no bro, about anything." I see a little sparkle in his eye and then it fades, as he thinks about it for a second, then replies, "they don't know what to care about."

What does the television tell you? Not much. And what it does tell you is only what it wants you to know. I just find it hard to believe that all news networks broadcast the same six stories every day as if it's the most important shit going on in the world. So, TV and the ones who dictate what's on it are obviously the enemy. Therefore, they're going to help out with the conversation so that leaves the most trusted, "word of mouth" to spread the message. Which is, hell, I don't even really know. Is it the fact that we think we are free when in reality we aren't? Or is it that our government is probably the most corrupt and oppressive in the world? Is it perhaps that what we've been conditioned to care about really doesn't mean shit? Now that I think about it; every single, god damn thing we've been told has been bullshit. Well, maybe not everything, but damn near everything. Hell, I guess it started off with Santa Claus, and ended up with us believing we were free in this fake ass land of liberty.

So, that's the message, or part of it at least, and I'm tired, so I decide to take a nap. "I dream and, in my dream, I hear a voice and it says to me,"

"How does my voice get heard if not by your mouth?"

And I reply, "by someone else's mouth Lord."

And then the voice who I know is God almighty says, "Am I to write when you've nothing better to do?"

He got me on that one. And I admit so by saying, "I get the point."

So, the scene in the dream is simple, but I'll explain so you have an idea. I'm standing, and all is dark around me except for me and the light above me that is illuminating me and a small circumference around me. The voice came from above. I assume it and the light emanates from the same source. So, after the last dialog, I know what I'm to do, but I have a sense of doubt, or perhaps fear, possibly a bit of both. My God, who knows, all goes on to say, "Do not be afraid and do not waver in your beliefs. My judgment is coming to a wicked and perverse nation. They turn from me and now trust in their riches. They've kept the poor from justice and excused the rich in court. They deny what is good and accept what is wrong. My hand is against them, and just as then, so is now. The tools I choose to use. You will be my writing hand, and my words will flow from your mouth. Be brave, be true, and let your heart be your guide. Don't fear death as it comes to all. Let your work pay you with eternity instead of cash. Understand the mysteries of the world and stand up to evil. I am your guide, and I am with you."

The sound of, "Sleep late lose weight!" brings me back to reality. It's supper time. Tonight's course is a fine delicacy consisting of cornbread, mixed vegetables, a piece of cake and rice with mystery meat again. Fuck my life. I eat it with thanks though, and sprinkle some noodle seasoning on the main course and vegetables which helps the palate, but not the blood pressure. We eat, and as usual the floor is open to trades, but I don't try my hand at any souls. As usual we stack our trays by the door, and proceed to our usual activities, and as usual, I'm left to my thoughts.

My thoughts! My thoughts! My thoughts! So, if the dream was a vision, it answers the question of whether or not God is on our side. This is a great confidence booster, because if God be for us who can be against us. The fucked-up part is I know that all throughout history the men and women who wrote and spoke God's word were persecuted, tortured, imprisoned, and most were eventually killed. The irony is they were hated while alive, but immortalized after their deaths by their words being published in their figures carved out of iron, stone, bronze, gold, or any other material man had the ability to shape. Their message fell on deaf ears until they were killed for it, and then the people understood. Why, oh why, do we not see until it's too late? Why must we hear with our ears and not understand with our hearts? Why do we despise what is good and believe the lies of the evil? After dinner I sleep, because I don't feel like playing cards and I usually feel dumber after watching TV.

I am not a huge fan of sleep, but on the inside, it kills time, and sometimes that is the objective. I do not believe what the doctors say. We were told we need eight hours a day. If my calculations are correct, if you sleep eight hours a day, and live to be seventy-five, you will have slept twenty-five years of your life away. One third of your life is spent asleep while those with sinister intentions plot and scheme. If you're sleeping, you can't be doing much thinking, and that's precisely what they want, for you to do as you're told, believe what they say, and never question or think about your current situation, which is bleak at best, but hopefully we can do something about it.

I wake up in the middle of the night to take a piss. As always, people are up. Some are on cell phones, others smoking weed or spice. I'm just trying to take a piss and go back to sleep. I figure this will be my last weekend at this facility since I just got sentenced. My time here is done. I'm out of the way letting others do as they may. I've grown fairly insensitive to noise or being awakened in the middle of night for whatever reason it may be. As I said, we adapt quickly. So, I piss next to a guy sitting in a urinal dangling his feet like he is on a pier. He is obviously high out of his mind. So, I nod politely, shake my dick a couple of times, and go wash my hands. Then it's back to my rack and back to sleep.

Then it hits me, and for a moment I'm lost, but realize it's just the fluorescent lights blinding and discombobulating me. I know it's time for the 6:00 AM certified count. We've got a feisty little CO working this morning and she comes in doing her job. She is moving people's tents back, and throwing them on the floor, waking everyone up saying, "let me see your eyes." She checks us all off of her list. She ain't but about 5'2 with "high yellow" skin as they say. Most of these guys can't control their lust over her, and she knows and likes it. Even though she is cute, ain't none of those fools happy about being woken up by her abuse of authority, and they are all very verbal about their feelings. It doesn't faze her though. It's Saturday, and she probably has a hot date tonight, and quite possibly had a bad one last night, which is why she came in on the bullshit. It makes no difference to me. I sit here passively as they all talk shit to one another. I'm just ready for my breakfast. We get cereal and milk on Saturday, and I love milk.

Bran flakes with no raisins, my favorite. Not really, but as I said, I love milk. Two biscuits and some white gravy with a little sausage in it. I truly am thankful for this meal just as I am all meals. I actually score myself two extra milks for a cigarette each. Myself and the other parties involved both feel as if we won. That's the way the barter system is supposed to work. Now that I've got myself some milk, I can spruce up my instant freeze-dried Colombian crack; two rounded spoons of the freeze-dried gold, one milk, two sugar substitutes, and a smashed-up fireball. If I had some hot chocolate, I'd add a scoop as well. But what I've got will do just fine. So, I stir the mixture then make my way to the microwave to bring it all to a boil. Afterwards, back to my rack to enjoy something better than any coffee shop has and one of the cheapest cigarettes on the market. Fuck my life!

The coffee is good, and the cigarette is even better, which makes me think. Tobacco is allowed at this facility, but where I'm headed next it isn't. I wouldn't be doing my job if I didn't try, and besides, what are they going to do, lock me up if I get caught? So, I began to weigh my options. I am almost certain on Monday morning I'll be leaving here. I can try and smuggle some brown "aka tobacco" with some of my commissary items, or I can use the trusty old penitentiary safe deposit box, "aka-asshole." Decisions! Decisions! Decisions! Although I've now got over five years under my belt in the penal system, my butt is still a virgin to foreign objects. It is the safest route, but this is a huge moral decision that one must make. I could try both routes, which would increase the payload and double my chances of success, but I'm still not comfortable with the whole idea of wrapping tobacco with cling wrap and then inserting it into my butt. I may have to sleep on this one.

As usual, after breakfast when they give the announcement for yard call, most of the guys have gone back to sleep. It will be about ten more minutes before the CO's actually come down to let us out. So, I suppose they made the announcement because they suspect all those who want to go will be up and ready by then. They are wrong, because no one has moved although they all heard the message over the intercom system. So, I sit back and observe, and I wait for what I know is coming. And then it happens, in pops a guard walking through the door and yelling, "Yard Call!" Now we have movement. Although it's not rushed or in a hurry, we have movement, as guys start getting out of bed, brushing teeth, putting on shoes, making a cup of coffee, all the while yelling, "hold that door we coming." This shit is hilarious to me, and it's the same shit everywhere. Finally, ten minutes later, the CO came into our unit to take us to the yard. They are finally moving towards heading out. I opted to stay in because I'm comfortable and don't feel like going out and getting sweaty.

It may seem strange to you but if you've never been in my

shoes, it wouldn't. Once you accept one of these places as your home, you really don't want to leave unless you're leaving for good. You get comfortable with the place and the people around you. A secure feeling begins to slowly creep over you. This feeling is what prevents me from going to the yard this morning, and it is the same reason I was so ready to get back here after court. Maybe I am institutionalized. Or, once again maybe I'm bat-shit crazy. I guess only time will tell, or perhaps you can be the judge by the time you finish reading this.

All is quiet now as some are asleep, and the rest of my little angels have gone outside to terrorize anything insight. I once again get to think about the vision I had from God. From my own understanding, I had already put together the pieces of the puzzle that form the relationship between man and God. Although it's very blurry, I can make out the basic outline of how it works. God is the energy force that drives everything, is in everything, and created everything. In essence God is everything collectively, but individually everything is not God. I've also learned if you act according to the will of God, most everything around you will help in the mission, since God is in everything. There is opposition though. We have free will, which means we can choose to serve our own purpose or follow God's will. Many a good man have given their lives in order to serve God's will and the trick will be preserved life and still serve the Lord, and still make it through this shit into retirement age. Fuck my life!

Then it hits me, I'll just write a fictional novel about some real ass shit, and although the people are far from having freedom of speech, artist can write, say, or express themselves however they deem fit. Because you can't bridle art, or it wouldn't be art. I mean if Picasso had been forced to paint flowers instead of what he wanted to paint, would his heart have been in it? And if your heart isn't in it, will it end up being the best you can do? Of course not. Anything you do should be done wholeheartedly, or it will be subpar at best. In my situation though, this venue is the only one left with enough freedom to say what needs to be said and not end up with an accidental bullet in the back of one's head.

A book will converse with more people than I could ever find time to. It will speak when I'm dead and gone. It will prevent fools from arguing about this or that detail and missing the whole point, and I can say it's all fiction. So, I need to buy some writing pads and pens and start putting this shit together.

The rest of the day, that night, and Sunday all passed uneventfully, and now I'm back to my smuggling operations. I have two jars of peanut butter. I scoop the contents out and place my carefully wrapped tobacco inside. I melt the peanut butter and pour it back into the jars after it cools. It looks just like it came straight from the factory. I'm still undecided on the old keister. I will sleep on it one more night and make the decision in the morning. I know they will transport me around 9:00 AM since that's what they always do. Their patterns aren't hard to track.

Then all hell breaks loose! Two members of the same gang have started trying to kill one another. One has a Shank made out of a piece of angle iron from one of the lights. He has sharpened and put a wrist lanyard on it and the other has one of the indestructible trays they feed us on. They are surely trying to take one another's lives. Although outgunned, the one with a tray has more heart and is whooping the hell out of the guy with the knife. Everyone is keeping their distance as this is an interdepartmental matter, and therefore none of your business, unless you are in the same gang as theirs. Then things take a turn for the worse. Someone breaks a sprinkler head off and the unit is flooding. This is the beginning of a riot, and I already know my role. Therefore, I pull out my cigarette lighter and a roll of toilet paper, light the latter and throw it as far as I can, just like in the movies.

I'm not certain if that was the best move, but it seemed so at the time. It did incite or inspire the rest of the guys into flooding toilets and setting more shit on fire. I mean hell, what do we got to lose? The scene is intensifying, and I can't remember ever having laughed so hard. Chaos is enthralling, but short lived. We aren't designed to keep up with it for long. Therefore, chaos comes and then moves on just as fast as it came, while we are left to clean up the mess.

After we had our fun and calmed down, the cops finally decide to come in. They know better than to come when we are all agitated and working together. So, they come in and act like they are running the show. Again, we are all soaked, as well as them, and the sprinkler system is still doing its job. They don't have enough cells to put us all in, so the worst they can do is turn off the TV, take away visitation and our commissary. I really don't give a fuck about any of it because I know I'm leaving in the morning.

The guards are pissed though, they throw all of our shit on the floor where there was just enough water on it to soak everything. Then they strip search us four at a time. I decide to use this opportunity to talk shit to the guard and ask him,

"Is this your Favorite part of the job?" I point out my tattoo while squatting for him. He just snarls and says, "turn around, squat, and cough." Lucky for him I had a bowel movement a couple of hours earlier. So, the best I can do is say, "Oh, your favorite part is this, how's your dad feel about you being gay?" The other three guys getting stripped searched laugh like hell at this, and I get electrocuted with the Taser. Apparently, my bowels weren't quite as empty as I thought because I actually shit myself a little bit when the electricity pulsed through my body. It wasn't much though, and well worth the comment. I do feel as if I won that battle because I'm pretty sure the guy was really gay and that his father was highly disappointed in him. The pain he inflicted on me is already gone, while he has to live with himself every day.

By the time they get out of our zone and leave us the hell alone, it's way past midnight. They mixed everyone's shit up, which is a tactic they use to try and get us to kill one another, but it doesn't work. We had too much fun in our mini riot to be bothered by their dumb shit. Even the two guys who were trying to kill one another have shaken hands and made up. We have peace on earth. Well, except for the Holy Land, part of Africa, any place our military is wreaking havoc and the US Mexican border. Well, at least we've got it in our zone.

I'm exhausted by the time I hit my bunk and fall asleep instantly. Again, I'm blinded as the god damn fluorescent lights, signifying a convict's sunrise and another day in the jungle. The concrete jungle that is. I fire up a smoke and wait for these folks to come count us and then serve us our breakfast. It would be nice if they would bring it to us on our racks, but that may be asking a little much. I would hate to come off seeming entitled. If you think about it though, they wash our clothes, pay the cable bill, clothe and house us, and all we've got to do is eat, sleep, shit, and be a pain in the ass as often as we can. Recidivism.

We ate breakfast, which you should have guessed was oatmeal and some biscuits. I've yet to decide on "keistering" some tobacco for the upcoming drought in the next facility. I am by no means gay, and don't believe either of the sayings, "It's not gay as long as you leave your socks on", or "You can't tell the difference with your eyes closed", both of which have probably worked on countless individuals, but neither of which seemed like truth the more I reflect on it. I'm questioning whether it's morally OK to be a man and shove something up my ass when the police come in with a cart call my name and tell me to pack. They make the decision for me. Thank God!

3 A New Day

With my manhood still intact, and my pride still with me, I throw all my shit in a laundry bag, all while fighting off those pesky prison vultures who never speak to someone until they are leaving. It is only in hopes of grabbing something that is being left behind. You've got to be very careful, and even more watchful, when they swoop in on you. So being that I'm surrounded and outnumbered, I resort to showing my teeth and growling to keep them at bay. It works, and I get my few worldly possessions shoved into a laundry bag and hoisted over my shoulder before saying my goodbyes and shaking hands with a few good men.

After that I'm off to see the emerald city, I mean my county jail, to deal with still pending charges that I just received my first sentence for. The inside of the jail does remind one of the "Emerald City" because they chose a somewhat hideous green colored stucco for the interior walls. I'm not sure if it has a psychological effect or if the interior designers just had bad taste. Either way, I'm ready to get back and get this next step over with.

The van ride is a quick one, and I once again find myself ready to be where I'm going and out of society. The sun is shining, and I find that it hurts my eyes. I also notice the color of my skin is almost translucent. Perhaps my frequent stents will prevent me from getting skin cancer in my older years. Next, I'm sitting in booking with an officer in no hurry to do her job. Patience is a virtue I've somewhat developed. So, I just sit and wait. I've got all my belongings with me, and she is eyeballing it like she does not feel like going through all of it. What more would you expect out of a $14.00 an hour employee though? I've no fear of her finding my hidden contraband. Perhaps it's my life of crime that has taught me to keep my cool when breaking the law. Or perhaps it's the fact that I don't see what I'm doing or what I've done wrong. I know the consequences if caught, and I know it's against the law, but wrong? No, not wrong, just against the rules. I mean, think about it; is it really wrong if I sneak more tobacco from one jail to another? Is God going to judge me for this? I certainly hope the Lord's view of right and wrong is higher than this. If not, I'll just have to stand in front of the judgment seat with a clear conscience and defend my case.

I sit and wait, she looks at me, I look at her, she looks at my bag and then pretends to be busy typing on the computer. This goes on and on for I don't know how long. Finally, a Sergeant walks in that I know. Most of the officers know me because I was here just weeks ago. The Feds came and got me just long enough to sentence me, then brought me back. So, I ask the sarge if he will put me back in the pod I came out of, and he nods. Then the booking lady tells him she doesn't want to go through my stuff. After a quick glance at my bag, I can tell he doesn't want too either. Once again what more could you expect out of a $19 an hour employee?

The Sarg calls me back to the priest's chambers, I mean the dressing room, where I'm a good little altar boy, I mean inmate, and strip, squat, and cough in such a hurry, and faster than he can get the words out of his mouth. He looks and gives me the okay to put my clothes back on. We walked out sharing a sacred bond with one another. I wonder if the Nazis shared the same bond with all the Jews they persecuted?

Probably so, they probably used that classic line, "I'm just doing my job." Fuck it, I'm shameless now after having countless men view my genital and butthole, each time taking a little piece of me away, and now there just isn't much more to take.

As we walk back into the booking room, he takes another glance at my bag, then asks the booking lady, "You haven't searched his stuff?" She says, "Uh, I got too much to do on the computer, you go through it." He is shaking his head as another CO walks in. The Sarg looks at him and says, "Take him to F-Pod." I look at the Sarg and say, "What about all my shit?" He looks at me and says, "We'll put it in your property until someone gets a chance to go through it, then we will bring it to you." Well, I knew right then that was a fucking lie, and I won't never be getting my shit. It's a battle I know can't be won though. So, I accepted my defeat and walked with the officer to my new old home.

Walkin in the pod, I see most of the same guys who were here when I left a month or so ago. This place is a polar opposite as far as the way it is set up from the place I just left. There are two floors of cells, six up top and six on the bottom holding a total of twenty-four men. I say my hellos to the guys I know, throw my mat on the top bunk in a cell with an old friend, and settle in to catch up on all the latest gossip. Ain't too much happened in my absence, besides the usual, a couple of fights. The jail is almost full, and we now have a "lady boy" living in the pod with us. I explain to everyone how the Feds gave me eighteen months to run consecutively with whatever sentence I'm about to receive from the state. Everyone says, "That's some bullshit!" and I agree. I then tell my celly that if they bring me my shit, I've got some blessings hidden inside. This is good news for him, as we are in a nonsmoking facility now, and security is tight. That means contraband is hard to come by. The less contraband, the more hostile the environment, because when people have nothing to lose, giving a fuck gets thrown out of the window.

Once again, I have nothing except the two pairs of socks I wore here from the last facility as well as the three pairs of boxers. I knew to do this because I could foresee them not giving me my property. Call me an old convict if you will, but I know how these folk's work. So, I've got my socks, my boxers, one blanket, one mat, and that's it. I'm going to have to harass every officer I see to get a roll of toilet paper, toothbrush, toothpaste, a bar of soap, a towel, and a rag. That's just how it is here. I kinda wish I would have shoved a pack of tobacco up my ass. It's Monday, the canteen comes on Friday, and they pull the orders on Wednesday night so by Wednesday my mother, the rock of my life, will have some money on my account, and by Friday I'll at least have something in my box to eat if I get hungry.

I was doing good out there before a breakup caused a treacherous woman to steal from me, fabricate false kidnapping and rape charges on me, and try and have my life ruined or ended by a shootout with the cops or land with a life sentence behind bars, all of which my God shielded me from. Besides that, though I was doing good. I was running my own company and had a little money put back with which my mother has been using to pay my child support and send money to my commissary account. I couldn't ask my family to support me through this financially. This will be my second trip to prison, and they looked out for me the first time. When the money is gone, it's gone. More motivation.

You see, all paths lead to this book of course. I have a choice; I could watch TV, play cards, exercise, or talk shit all day long like all these other guys, but in the grand scheme of things, what good will that do me or anyone else for that matter? Not one single bit, that's how much! Life, and our sense of time, are valuable things and very easy to waste and let slip by before you know it. Take being incarcerated for instance, doing time seems to take forever. Looking back on it, it passed in the twinkle of an eye. I'm thirty-six, and eighteen seems like just a few days ago. My life is either at its halfway point or very close to it. What have I dedicated it to? Getting high, making money, chasing women. All for what? Two boys are all I have to show for it. And what am I doing for them now? I'm trying to start a movement, that's what I'm doing!

The hardest part is going to be that there is something more important than sports, money, sex, or whatever advice it is they have. Freedom. All of those are encompassed under the umbrella of freedom, but so is so much more. If we were free milk wouldn't be five dollars a gallon because career politicians wouldn't exist. Actually, no politicians would exist. Every law they write is another pen stroke against freedom. It's amazing to think about how something paid for with the blood is destroyed with ink and paper. That is a god damn shame. That is a beautiful line. Thank God for it, not me. Perhaps in the same way they are destroying our freedom will these words you are reading find a way to redeem it.

For the here and now though, I need an extra blanket, a

pillow, and of course the toiletries the jail was supposed to provide for me, but didn't. My neighbor is the seamster in the zone and has fastened himself a needle out of a piece of copper wire from the busted light in his room. It has been folded down to form an eye window into one end after being beaten somewhat flat. Talk about lemon into lemonade. This fellow and I negotiated a price for the blanket and pillow for seven ramen noodles. I take the blanket with me while he starts making my pillow. My word is my bond, and he knows I'm good for it and will pay him Friday when the store comes.

Back in my cell, I was tying one blanket around my mat for a sheet when my celly comes in saying, "Coffee is in this container and noodles are down there if you get hungry." I thank him and carry on about my business. I'll probably take him up on the offer for some coffee between now and Friday, but probably not any noodles. I hate owing anyone, and the interest rate in here is crazy. It is two for one, meaning anything you get you owe two in return. I'll do without it before I pay that much interest. It never fails though in every unit, zone, or pod, you've got a store man, and then you've got people who start out in debt and never have the self-discipline to climb out. They eat fifty dollars' worth of stuff during the week and pay the store man one hundred dollars' worth on store day, only to repeat the cycle over and over again. I just can't bring myself to do it. I reckon this is no different from people living off their credit cards and working to pay the interest only to fall further and further into debt.

After making my bed and a cup of complimentary coffee, I walk out into the day room for a game of cutthroat. It's basically spades, each man for himself, instead of teams. My competition is stiff. I mean good enough. I've seen men end up with a final score of negative seventeen by the time the winner reached thirty. At the table is my new celly, my old celly from before I left, and the lady boy. Come to find out my old celly and the lady boy are cell mates now. This seems somewhat strange, but I don't give it too much thought as the card game is occupying my mind at the time. The most pressing conversation is about plea deals the public defenders have offered us and whether or not we are willing to accept or try for another one. My old celly got offered twenty years and is going to accept it. He already signed the deal, and is just waiting to stand before a judge. Everyone is focused on getting the gay guy on every hand he bids, so I end up winning the game. It was entertaining, but it was enough for me for a while. I decided to see if I can get my property brought to me. The fellas tell me they haven't had a cigarette in here in over a month. So, if my pack comes through it would be a godsend.

After pushing the button that links the speaker to the central tower, and getting lied to, I see a guard in the hallway. I shake the door as hard as I can to get his attention, and he walks over to open the door to our pod. I explained my situation and he says he will check on it and get back with me. Another lie. But at least I tried, and will continue to.

I ate lunch, which was shit, while I was up in booking, and now it's dinner time. I'll only have to tell you once what dinner is because it's the same motherfucking thing day in and day out. Supper here consists of four slices of white bread, two slices of bologna, one slice of cheese, two baby carrots, a piece of celery, two packs of mustard, three duplex cookies, and a four-ounce apples juice box. That's a lot of words, but not much food. It's what we get, and it is what it is.

So, we all lined up to get our bags and wouldn't you know it, someone didn't get theirs. So here comes the bullshit. The guard comes in and makes everyone come out of their cell, does a head count, says that's how many bags he put in here, and turns around and walks out. That is how concerned they are with whether or not you eat. You better not be a pussy cause you might go hungry. I wish it were different, but that is exactly how it is. The door slams behind the guard, and opinions are forwarded. No one owns up to stealing the old man's dinner, and a youngster gives him his bag. Then everyone splits into their different factions.

A couple minutes later the guy who gave up his dinner, and three other members of his gang, muted the TV and called everyone out into the day room. It doesn't look like they are going to let this shit ride. And they shouldn't. Court is adjourned, and the guilty party is going to get fucked up. Everyone here knows who took the bag. Now it's just a matter of finding out whether or not he is going to admit to it. Either way, it's going to be his ass, because they waited long enough to call this meeting that the fool has had time to eat it up. This in turn means he can't give it back, which in turn means four people are going to stomp on his ass until he is pumpkin headed, which is exactly what happened. The only sad part is the guy didn't have the nuts big enough to admit that he did it. So, he went down as a coward, and a thief. Here is the lesson of the day for you kids, never steal, especially while incarcerated.

That business has been handled and it's med pass time.

The nurse, her cart, and a CO are making their rounds passing out. Lord knows what kind of medicine. These guys are lining up in droves to take the shit. I guess I don't have to mention how they are peeping out the window, lusting over the nurse just as they do everywhere else. Hopefully you get the point about how that works by now. Anyhow, I sit back and watch as everyone gets their pills and walks back into the unit. Now starts the drug dealing.

There is one type of pill that has its outer layer peeled off, crushed into lines, and then snorted. I haven't tried any, but they say it gives you a rush, and the side effects is that it clogs the nasal cavity up for a while. Hey, whatever floats your boat man. I don't see any harm in it. I'd just wait for some good old cocaine if it were me. The real hot commodities on the market are the sleeping pills. The nurse makes the guys who take them open their mouths, lift their tongues and all of that bullshit, but what she fails to realize is they are just palming the pills and not even putting them in their mouth. It's entertaining to me, and the only way this could be better is if the door wasn't locked and I had a cigarette or a blunt.

Since I only like snorting cocaine and have never had a problem sleeping, I abstain from the illegal drug activities and watch a little television. They've got a preseason football game on, and when I see it, I lose my train of thought. For some reason the word, "Ball" comes to mind. Then I find myself thinking, "me and my friends are going to take this ball and move it across that line and ain't a damn thing ya'll can do about it." Then a commercial break comes on and I'm back to my senses, when suddenly the commercials are over, and all I can think of is "Ball." Fuck my life! This shit is going to be harder than I thought. Before I knew it, one of the teams took the ball across the line more times than the other, and scored more points, which means they won the game and I'm none the wiser from it.

I'm mentally exhausted after snapping out of the ball trance. I'm pissed off because they didn't let me keep my property. I moved into a new home today, so I decided to call it an early night. I ease into my cell, jump onto my top rack, and just as I drift off to sleep, my celly comes in and says he has to take a shit. Oh, the joys of a cell and a cellmate. I jump up though and make my way out of the cell. He says, "Sorry man." as I walk past, and I reply without turning around "I'd rather you do it now than after they've locked us down." He nods, pulls the door to, and goes on about his business. A couple minutes later he walks out and looks at me like, "I'm all done." I look at him like, "I'd like to stab you in the throat." Nothing like mutual understandings. I give it about ten minutes to air out then get back in bed and quickly fall asleep.

The motherfucker snores like a god damn grizzly bear and there is no doubt in my mind I now want to take his life with a homemade knife shoved into his neck many times over and over and over again. I woke up to take a piss, and now I'm just laying here listening to this fat fuck rumble, growl, and do his best to sound like an animal. Surely, we aren't meant to sleep like they say. I know one thing, tomorrow's focus will be on finding a new cell to stay in, and new celly. After calming myself and trying to forgive him for things he can't help, I finally fell asleep.

"Brrrrrrrrrr" is what jolts me out of my sleep here. It used to be the light in this facility as well, but they've all been busted out and the plexiglass and metal fashioned into shanks. The wires were snatched out and turned into stringers. So, a stringer is basically just two wires with a piece of metal attached to the end of each and the other of each wire connected to a hot source, and the other wire connected to the neutral. The pieces of metal are submerged into water, and when salt is added the current flows though the water completing the circuit and giving us boiling water. Since this place doesn't give us microwaves, we improvise, and therefore none of the cells have lights in them anymore. So instead of a flood of fluorescent light as an alarm clock, it's the electronic actuator that opens each cell door which is controlled by the tower. So, I rise, because as you should know by now, "You sleep late you lose weight." And I ain't trying to lose no weight.

A couple minutes later, trays are at our pod. And let me tell you, the food here fucking sucks, and I mean sucks. Out of all the places I've been, this one is by far the worst foodwise, treatment wise, and really just all-around worse jail I've ever been in. The breakfast consists of the same shit they give everywhere, else oatmeal or grits and biscuits, except the oatmeal here is more water than oats, no sugar of course, and the biscuits are not biscuits at all, but look like cornbread. They obviously just make huge square pans and then just cut serving size portions off. They are flexible and somewhat hard, which is pretty much exactly opposite of what a biscuit should be. Besides that, though, it's all the same. Guys are trading this for that, doubling back in line to get extra trays, and this is my life.

Everyone goes back to their cells and back to sleep after breakfast. My plans on moving out have been postponed. My celly is already snoring. I'm not tired, so I am not even going to attempt lying down. I've been doing time long enough to know how to sleep when you're tired, and don't even attempt it if you're not. If you are tired, they can be screaming, beating, rapping, snoring, or anything and you will sleep through it all. If you aren't tired, you blame all those actions, and the people behind them, for sleep evading you, which usually ends in conflict. And conflict is to be avoided at all costs because I'm not trying to black an eye or prove a point if it gets physical. I'm going to try my best to take my opponent's life, and that's something to be avoided if at all possible. So, I can't find a new cell just yet. So, it's time to turn my attention back to the hygiene products the jail was supposed to provide and the laundry bag full of my belongings I brought with me.

All the trays are stacked by the door, so I wait for my opportunity when I know the CO will be coming to collect them. I make my way towards the door when I hear the all too familiar rumble of the electronic lock operating. By offering a helping hand, I've opened up a short window to plead my case, and I choose the most important (toilet paper, towel, rag, soap, toothpaste, and toothbrush) over the bag I brought with me and say, "Man I ain't got no toilet paper, a towel, or none of that shit." He looks at me like I may be trying to get one over on him and says, "They didn't give you none of that?" So truthfully, I just look at him like, "Come on bro." I didn't' say a word, but he knew what I was saying and that I was telling him the truth. We finished loading the empty trays, and he says, "I'll bring you some stuff after I finish with all the trays." Finally, the truth! I nodded in a grateful manner and decided to go for a walk.

The dayroom is a triangle with three showers that have half walls on the opposite side of the cells, six four-man tables in the center arranged in a pyramid pattern, a flight of stairs, and three phones on one wall. I can either walk a straight line, turn around, and walk that line again, or I can make the block and walk all three sides. I decided on walking the triangle in a counterclockwise direction. I'm not sure why, but I always seem to find myself walking counterclockwise in these situations. Once again, I find myself walking like a hamster in a god damn wheel, steadily walking, but getting nowhere. I suppose it's better than sitting though. So, I walk, and I think. The latter brings me a bit of satisfaction, because if there is one thing a corrupt establishment does not want, one thing they fear, and one thing they can't control, is thinking. I promise you this, the American Government does not want the American Citizen thinking, unless it's about a mortgage, sports, buying groceries or any other bullshit. They do not want you to wonder why politicians own several multimillion-dollar homes, or federal judges own thousands of acres, and they somehow manage to do all of this on a humble public servant's pay. If you think or dig far into such matters, it may infuriate you and cause you to rise up with your neighbor and take your country back. You be a good person, and let them do what we can't do. Believe what they tell you, live by the laws they write, and shut the fuck up. I wonder when they split from, "we the people"?

Mankind is divided from within, separated by money, power, race, and creed, it was never meant to be. Too many different factions and philosophies all trying to overtake one another, and then you get what we have here today. A problem that everyone knows, but few seem to want to acknowledge, and even less want to talk about. Then a cell door opens in front of me, and it's just the man I want to see.

He is a friend who was also here when I left. He and I have had several intelligent conversations, and his IQ is definitely higher than the common ape. I looked at him with pleading eyes, and he invited me into his cell to talk. I explained my living situation, which he already knew. Everyone in the zone knew what kind of person my current celly is, as did I. But, in the rush of moving in, he said his cell was open, so I jumped in. Sometimes it's better to know what you've got instead of taking your chances and getting no telling what kind of cellmate.

We struck a deal for a bag of coffee on the store date for the bottom bunk. It's a blessing for the both of us, and I really appreciate him being a good person. Like I said, no matter what bad a man may do, there is always some good still in them. I don't necessarily mean my current cellmate as he is only here for a simple possession of meth charge. He is another victim of an unjust law. He worked, paid his bills, and liked to get high. What is so wrong with that? Not a god damn thing, that's what. If you've ever wondered what oppression means, this is a prime example. Let me elaborate if you will.

Imagine a world where everyone makes five-hundred dollars a week. Well, everyone except 1% of the population, who are the people in power and the super-rich. Everyone else makes five-hundred dollars per work week, and anytime they violate one of the countless laws, rules, or regulations they are with fined an entire week's pay, or perhaps more, depending on what the law says, or if they are imprisoned for a set amount of time. Now if you are fined a whole week's pay for speeding, two week's pay for not having insurance, one week's pay for not using your blinker, one year in prison for possessing over 30 grams of marijuana, two years in prison for possessing methamphetamine, and five years in prison for posing with a sawed off shotgun passed down in your family since the stagecoach days, how will the ninety-nine percent of the population who makes five-hundred dollars a week ever get out of the struggle and break free from the hand that keeps them down? They never will unless something changes. In reality they're the poor just working to work some more. If you didn't know or see this, you are forgiven. Now that you are fully aware, what's your excuse? I'll let you in on another secret; There is only one excuse in the whole wicked world, and to find it, all one must do is look in the mirror. And that is our lesson on oppression and excuses. Class is dismissed for the day.

Now it's feeding time, and as always, we line up, get our food, and open the floor for trades. Today's specialty is mystery meat patty, boiled noodles, no seasoning or cheese, mixed vegetables, cake, and hopefully, you guessed it, cornbread. Oh yeah, and grape juice pack. At least we are eating better than those little kids in Africa they always show on the commercials. The bastards don't even have the decency to wipe the flies off their little faces. So, I guess it could be worse, and perhaps that thought is what helps us hold on.

After lunch I informed my current cellmate of my newly acquired contract, and bottom bunk status, in the cell next to me. It's somewhat sad, as he looks like a child whose friend is moving to the next town. It's a touching moment, and if he weren't such a dickhead, didn't snore so loud, and could control his bowels, it may have worked out. But these are all negative attributes and only make life worse than it already is. Never be afraid to do what's best for you. So, I start moving, which only takes two trips, one to carry my mat and blankets, and the next my Bible. After a final sweep of the cell, I walked out, and left that place the same way I found it.

After settling in with my new celly, I make my way to the kiosk and send my momma a message, just telling her I love her. Then I pull up the commissary app and go down the list of essentials I need: deodorant, a bowl, a cup, coffee, noodles, and some aspirin for when a headache comes on. Thank goodness I had the foresight to wear two pairs of socks and three pairs of boxers from the last jail or that would be more money I'd have to spend on that. Then I realize I need a pen, paper, and some stamped envelopes. If I'm to make this shit happen, I'll need the tools of the trade. There go the couple extra bucks I was going to spend on the ingredients for a "sweet wrap" my celly and I were going to make. Oh well, priorities must come first. I've still got seven noodles, one for each night, my hygiene, a bowl, three bags of coffee and my pad and pen. Who knows what the last two may lead to.

After placing my order, I make my way back towards my cell, and then it hits me. I've got to take a shit and they've yet to give me my toilet paper. So, instead of the cell I head toward the door that allows entrance to and from our world. There is one surefire way to get some attention inside and that is to kick on the door as hard as you possibly can until someone wakes from their nap and decides to come see what the fuck your problem is. That is the plan, and just as I approach the door, it buzzes and there is the guard from earlier. What does he have in his hands? My toilet paper, towel, soap, toothpaste, and toothbrush. Talk about right on time!

I asked my celly if he needed anything out of the cell and informed him of my intentions of feeding the toilet. He makes himself a cup of coffee while I psyched myself up for being able to shit in private for the first time in weeks. You see, at the last facility it was an open bay with community toilets. Not here though. Every cell has its own stainless-steel throne with a sink built into it. So, just as my celly starts to walk out I'm overcome with the fear of being alone. I look at him with the saddest puppy dog eyes I can muster and say, "hey celly?" He stops mid stride, halfway in and halfway out of the door, and seeing the sincerity in my eyes asked, "What's up?" I take a deep breath and ask him, "Will you hold my hand?" He laughs a little and says, "If you need me to, I got you." as he walks out and shuts the door behind him. If you don't know, now you know.

I almost rigged up the hot water to stay on in the sink so that it drains into the toilet and heats the whole apparatus up. This creates a heated toilet seat and a steaming sensation on the butt. Nature is calling, and I don't have time for all that at the moment. Therefore, I just opt to enjoy the alone time. I do follow that golden rule of "down one, drown one" and before I know it my feet have fallen asleep. Now I'm faced with the real decision. Do I call my celly in for that helping hand or risk standing up on my own and potentially falling? If your feet have ever fallen asleep while you are sitting on the loo, you know how dangerous of a position I'm in. If you've never been in this position, I recommend you slow down, sit a little longer, and try this at least once before you leave this world. It truly is thrilling.

After wiping very diligently, just in case I fall, I decided not to use the buddy system and risk standing on my own. The pain shoots from my feet up into my calves, and I find myself laughing. I guess it's more of a painful pleasure. Almost as quickly as it came, it was gone. I put my clothes back on. I guess that sounds crazy to you that I was naked, but before you judge please let me explain.

Imagine, if you will, you're sitting on the toilet, minding your own business, shirt rolled up a bit onto your lower back, and pants and undies around your ankles. Let's say you're enjoying the latest interior design magazine, and the door opens behind you, and you holler out, "I'm shitting in here!" And then a deep voice replies, "I know." So, you turn around as far as you can without making a mess on the toilet seat and there stands Nasty Nate. He is big, he is black, and he is stroking his penis in a very menacing, not funny, kind of way. Now a fight or flight kicks in, but as you stand you fall, because your pants are around your ankles. Now you are a fish out of water. Next, he grabs your shirt and pulls it over your head and begins to deflower you in an animalistic kind of way. This is no good folks, and it's for this reason I get naked when I take a poo.

Back in reality, I opened the door to my cell and made my way out into the day room. It's the same old scene, guys playing cards, and guys watching TV. I walk around for a little while, and since there ain't shit going on, I decide it's time for a shower. Hygiene is a must up in here. The guys don't let that shit slip by. Everyone knows when everyone else showers, and everything else about everyone else up in here. It's all we have to watch, besides TV. Why do you think I know myself and others so well? It's because I have two eyes, and I use them to observe my surroundings and my fellow beings.

So, I grabbed the soap. Contrary to popular belief, it doesn't come with a rope. I also grab my towel and rag, then make my way to center stage. I say that because the three showers are in the center wall, right in the middle of the unit. With only a waist high wall it's prime time for the shower sharks to start patrolling. Don't be alarmed if you haven't heard of this species. They can't be found off the coast of Florida or any of the oceans in the world. But they can be found in every local county jail. They patrol with lustful eyes every time someone decides to wash their ass. I used to be bothered about the thought, but over time I've developed the mindset of a high-class stripper. You can look just not touch, and I do accept donations in the form of noodles and honeybuns.

These showers suck because you can't just turn a knob and the water stay on. They have a push button that turns the water on for 30 seconds at a time, and then you've got to push it again. Apparently, they don't want us wasting water or getting too comfortable in the shower. The way we work it out is this; we are patient enough to push the button as many times as we want, and the hot water never runs out. So, who really won that battle? Humans are so resilient, and we can find the best in any situation. These are things you can only learn by being down, by being despised, by being all alone, and by being in here. While I'm washing my ass I spot the first shower shark up on the top tier, and I immediately face the predator and start washing the genitalia. This tactic acts as a deterrent to all except the most vicious of the creatures who get off on the front or backside. Luckily the one on top is of the more tamed type and walks off after we make eye contact. I am able to finish my shower, dry off, and head back to my cell to adorn my red and white stripes.

While sitting on my bunk, I think about this madness, and thank my God that I can't see, and don't know, all that goes on behind closed doors in this world. This time is a blessing and a curse, because one has time to ponder on such matters. I may also be a curse for me because I HAVE to think about all these things. It would be much easier if I could just watch TV, think about women, or how to get over on the next man as so many do. Not me, I'm cursed to think about reality, about corruption in high places, about God and the duality of man. Perhaps one is better off just focusing on making money for the bills, believing what they are told, and thinking the justice system really represents justice. Then I wish, for just a moment, I could be like that, before realizing "I was" at one point in time. I then think, "I know I'd never go back even if I could."

Just before my thoughts carry my feet off the ground, I hear the feeding call, and make my way towards the door with the rest of the sheeple. I've already told you what dinner consists of here every single day. If you don't remember I don't feel sorry for you. So, I walk up, grab my bag, and make my way back towards my cell without any trading. All I'm concerned with is eating right now even though I'm not really hungry. It's dinner time, so that means it's time to eat, right? Wrong! I'm only supposed to eat when I'm hungry. not when I'm told to. This thought makes me feel like a wretched fool, and I decide to save my food for later. Battles such as this may seem insignificant or perhaps even foolish to you, but I can assure you, every battle won is not one lost, if that makes sense to you.

My good old celly walks in and asks if everything is OK, and I just nod. In reality it's not. I feel as if I'm wrongfully imprisoned and being dealt with unjustly. Perhaps I'm wrong. I've been that before, but the way I see it is, if it ain't wrong it shouldn't be illegal. The only thing I view as wrong is to harm someone who doesn't deserve it. When I say this, I mean everything concerning a person including their property, but excluding their feelings. We can't live in a physical world ruled by every single individual's feelings. Everyone feels different, and that shit has no place in our civilization. Don't steal. Don't kill. Don't rape, and don't manipulate, pretty much sums it up. I guess I'm just a simpleton concerning the fact. I believe we should live a life based on what's right or wrong, poor simple fool that I am.

This shit is exhausting. I don't know how much time I'm going to get for my victimless crimes against the country of America. The deputies have told me I'm to get two years, but until the plea is signed, and the judge drops the hammer, anything is possible. This may not sound like a lot, or it may sound like an eternity to you. In reality, based off of our legal system, it is a blessing. This is only because a wicked woman falsely accused me of kidnapping and rape. Since they didn't do anything to her for lying and filing a false police report, their conscious made them feel pity for me, and therefore only decided to give me two years instead of ten or twenty. If that ain't justice, I don't know what justice is. To ruin someone's life, or at least try to, only to receive a good cursing out, while the other is taken from family, children, and society, seems like an equal payout to a blind fool. My only hope is that a just God, who cares nothing for social status, sex, what type of clothes a person wears, or what unjust laws written by unjust people say, will take up my case and see to it that wrongs are righted and the wicked pay for their deeds. What do we have without hope?

Hopefully, this helps to explain the blessing and curse of having time to think. I wish you had it yourself. Not in this environment of course, but in a peaceful, comfortable setting of your own choosing. This would be possible for all of us if we weren't caught up in the devil's snare of focusing on money, and all the worldly cares. We must find a way to break these bonds. What's going on is far from new, it's been going on since the beginning. The only difference is the faces. Who is to know if we aren't even the same old souls repeating a meaningless life over and over until one day or one life, something clicks. We begin to understand with our heart instead of our brain. We see with our mind instead of our eyes. We begin to live instead of existing. Then it all changes, whether it be because God ordained it, or our choices allowed it. I don't know, but it changes. You feel cheated and deceived and wronged by the whole world, only to finally understand, they know not what they do. Then you realize it's not people who are the enemy, but an established system of evil that runs the world. Men are simply pawns in a much grander game than we realize. Then once again you are faced with a choice just like you have been your whole life. The only difference is this choice can either make you whole or split your soul into. Do you stand alone against all the darkness of the universe, or do you cower down and destroy yourself from within?

I've made the choice, and I don't think I need to tell you what path I took. I wish it were commissary day because after all this thinking I've come up with plenty to write. It's Tuesday right now though, and the store won't be here until Friday afternoon. A short time for you and only the twinkle of an eye when looked back upon, but in here, with not much else to look forward to, it may as well be an eternity.

4 The Plea

It's ten o'clock and lockdown time for us bad boys. So, the guards come in and tell us what we already know while yelling out, "Lockdown! Everyone to their cells." Then someone yells back, "Hell no! We won't go!" They are just talking shit, but it gets everyone a little roused. One of the guards shuts the door to our zone. They usually just leave it pulled to. Whether he thought we were serious, or he just did it by accident, he shut it. Now you hear shouts of, "Y'all in here with us now." All in good fun though. Once they make it to our cell, they call out my celly's name, and then ask me what I'm doing in here. I just look at them and say, "I thought this is where I was supposed to be." Which technically isn't a lie because I do feel like it's where I'm supposed to be. He looks at his roster sheet and says, "No you ain't. You're supposed to be in the next cell over." Now is my chance to have a little intellectual fun, so I say to him, "But it feels so right over here." He kind of looks at me and says, "the paper says you belong in that other cell, not this one." He couldn't have said a more perfect sentence because my reply will hopefully end the conversation and secure my new cell. So, I say to him, "does it mean it's right just cause the paper says so? What about what my heart feels?" Now is the moment of truth, and whether it be because he believed it and I got the higher point, or because I've stumped him and rose to a higher level than he was capable of reaching, he says, "Whatever. I'll change it in the computer. Y'all have a good night." then slams the door and walks to the next cell. Mission accomplished.

We shared a laugh and victory cupcake each before drifting off to sleep. Another check mark in the win column, and a bottom bunk to boot. They may have my body, but my mind is far from them. I should probably thank them for giving me the time to think for myself and hopefully help others view things in a new light. With the shoe on the other foot, and with a little more understanding, I thank God for it all. As soon as the door buzzes. I open my eyes the next morning. Grits, two pieces of white bread, scalloped potatoes, two packs of sugar and a grape juice pack is the all-star breakfast for Wednesday morning. I chew and swallow, as taste is not needed or wanted for such a meal, and then head back to the cell to sleep, hopefully until right at ten in the morning, which is what time lunch comes.

I just as I fell asleep, I'm awoken by someone calling my name out in the day room. I'm in no hurry because there just ain't no need to be in a hurry. I get up and open my cell door to see who's calling my name and interrupting my beauty sleep. It's a CO at the door and he says, "Put on your uniform, you've got a lawyer visit." Oh joy! Now comes the part where I sign my life away, because to go to trial means to get the maximum sentence on my charges. That's their way of deterring anyone from going to trial. Plus, I am guilty of the drug and gun charges. So, I brush my teeth, adorn my rags, or rather uniform, and finally make my way out towards the guard. Then, out in the hallway, I face the wall and methodically raise my feet one at a time for him to shackle me up. I know the routine, and outwardly I am the ideal inmate, but inwardly is a whole different story. We make our way down a long hallway towards the central control and then take a right. We then walk up to a door that unlocks at our approach, and then walk towards the attorney client rooms. Once again, the door unlocks at our approach and the guard leaves, as I enter the room where my attorney is patiently waiting.

She is sitting opposite a table with files and papers neatly stacked on it. She is overworked and probably underpaid as a public defender. But nonetheless she does what she can. I'm not certain, but I believe she must have some sense of wanting to fight the machine to have chosen the career path she did. Of course, she knows some get exactly what they deserve, but she also knows that many get the shaft. In a previous conversation of ours, I quoted the laws and proceeding regarding a preliminary hearing and a release on recognizance bond, to which she informed me, "That wouldn't apply to my case." I wasn't surprised at this, as I know full well this shit ain't nothing like the tv shows. So, my reply to her statement was, "That's about right. I know the law only applies to those who "they" want it too." She gave me that look that I seem to get a lot that says, "You aren't supposed to say things like that." It didn't bother me though because I've always known my burden, but only recently decided to bear it. Anyhow, that was the past, and this is the present, and it's time to get down to business and cut a deal.

So, the sheriff's department kept their word, and the plea deal is what they said it would be, two years served and five years' probation, afterwards. Woo-hoo! That means I'll be serving three years and let me tell you, I'm ecstatic. Not really, but it sounded good. I signed the papers, and thanked my attorney for all her assistance, and then asked when I'll go before the judge. She answers, "on the first available open docket." This dims my spirit, and my face obviously expresses my feelings because she instantly asks, "What's wrong?" I look at her and reply, "Next week marks six months that I've been locked up, and not once have I been able to see my children. I'm ready to get this over so I can be moved somewhere that allows visitors under eighteen and contact visits. I'm tired of seeing my family behind a glass and only being able to video chat with my sons. I know how backed up the courts are and that it may be week or more until I can get in front of a judge."

In no way was I trying to manipulate her or my position on the list. I was simply speaking the truth from my heart, and she knew it. Therefore, she said, "I'll see what I can do." That ended our meeting, and just like that I knew my fate. Well, there's always a chance the judge can choose not to accept my plea and sentence me to whatever he or she chooses, but ninety-nine percent of the time they accept the deal, and go with the flow. Thank goodness I'm not a judge, because apparently, I have a problem with going with the flow.

Back in the unit, I'm bombarded with questions from fellow inmates, not that they are nosey, on second thought they are. Either way, everyone wants to know where I went, who I spoke with, and then finally what the offer was. After feeding them what they all wanted, it's back to my cell for some somewhat alone time.

It's a fucked-up world we've inherited. That's for sure. The thought of how they won't let children visit their parents until they make it to prison and stop fighting the system. Or how county jail time is designed to break a man's spirit until he submits. They feed you shit. They make you wait months not knowing what your sentence will be, wreaking havoc on you and your loved ones. Then to think it's all meticulously designed this way is sickening and saddening. We are your sons, your brothers, your fathers, and friends and all because of a choice or a series of choices, this is what we are reduced to. We all see, hear, and know things aren't right, but for some reason have developed the mentality that as long as it's not happening to us, it's ok." That is a false doctrine if I've ever heard one, and I'm here to tell you that it is happening to you. It's happening to all of us, one lie, one law and one theft at a time. I'm not telling you anything you don't already know. You just don't have or haven't made time to think about that feeling that you have inside of you. It's time.

It is time to have intelligent conversations about things that matter instead of who won the game or what star is whoring themselves out to another star. It's time to see the homeless you drive by every day as people instead of objects. It's time to stand up for what is right no matter how large of a force wrong places in front of you. It's time to call liars, liars and crooks, crooks, even if they do wear $2000 dollar suits. If the police do wrong, then they, just as we, should be punished. It's time to wake up from the darkness evil has encompassed us in and be the lights we are supposed to be. It's time to be free and let our hearts guide us instead of the rich and powerful. It is time to live the way God designed it to be. Now I know the topic of that conversation I wrote of earlier. I just hope I can remember all this by the time my pen and paper arrive. God forbid I get distracted by a ball in the meantime.

5 Time

And just like that, time stopped, or at least came to a complete crawl. Our perception of time, in a purely mechanical way, has to be flawed. In the big picture, I'd say time doesn't truly exist, because there is no beginning and no end to everything. Here, in an 8x12, time is very real. Now that I have something to look forward to, even though I don't know when, time has pulled that same old trick it pulls on us as children. Remember the trip to the park, or a party or beach, or anywhere else you looked forward to going? Always, and I mean always, it took longer going than the trip home. Mean old father time! I must find some frivolous activity to occupy my mind. It's no use fighting it, so when time does this, you must find a way to do time.

Then, what do you know, a potential activity knocks on my door. It's the lady boy, and it's unfortunate for me, but I don't get down like that. Therefore, I decided to have a little non-sexual fun with him or her, which is what we call them sometimes. Not sure if I described him earlier, but I'll paint you a pretty easy picture. If you've known one you've known them all. You can tell that his hair was bleached blonde, but now it's grown out, so the brown is just as long as the blonde, and of course it appears oily. He is about the size of my pinky, but a little over 6' tall with a little pot belly that reminds me of a slim woman about five months along in her pregnancy. One thing is for certain though, that's not a baby, and I'm almost certain it's not because he hasn't been trying.

Anyhow, he asked me, "How are you?" and I reply that

I'm just fine, all things considered. I'm not really sure what his intentions are, especially since the only time we've spoken was at the card table. I am hoping his intentions are pure. I give him the benefit of the doubt. I told him time just slowed down, and I was about to find something to occupy my mind, when he walked in. He takes this completely wrong. So, I decided to take it and run. Just a little fun with him. So, I ask him, "is it true that you can't tell the difference as long as you keep your eyes closed?" I realized instantly that I probably shouldn't have said that to him. I can see that he has never thought about it like that, but now that he has, he will probably use it as a pickup line in the future. Hopefully, God won't hold me accountable for it if he uses that line to talk some poor innocent bastard into allowing him to syphon his soul out through his manhood. I don't know how I'd defend myself in front of the Almighty if he puts the shame on me.

Now that I have started the ball rolling, and can see the lust in his eyes, I do exactly what I'm supposed to do and fuel the fire. "It's all the same on the inside." He says and I can't keep myself from laughing. If there is one think I know it's bullshit, and that was bullshit. It's time to put a stop to the madness before it gets out of control. So, I tell him, "I'm just picking with you man, but don't be using my pickup line. I've got a copyright on it." Of course, now he thinks I'm playing and that I was serious earlier. Fuck my life! The air is getting a little thick in the cell, so I decided to move the conversation out into a well-lit public area.

I asked the little princess if she wanted to play cards, and she accepted my offer. Now we need two more players, and she is the perfect recruiting tool. So, I send her off to do what she does best, which is find victims. It doesn't take her long to find us two more players and before I know it, she has dragged her celly, and my old cell, out to the table. This should be an interesting game of cards. We decide on spades, and wouldn't you know it, "sugar britches" sits across from me, making him/her my partner. I give her a little wink as they deal out the cards and tell say, "Make daddy proud." Oh, she blushes at this comment. I catch a glance of the look her celly give her at my comment. It's one of those, "Bitch I'll kill you!" looks. I think to myself, "oh Lord have mercy." I know this will be a memorable game.

The cards were dealt, and since it's the first hand, we don't have a bid. Sugar britches and I ran a wheel on them, which means get ten books, which in turn means start a new game because we just won that one. Once again, I fulfill my role and talk shit. What makes this all the more hilarious is that the lady boy's celly is one of those macho men, "fuck you" types. It never fails that they are always the closet gays, just as the case is here today. Being who he is, he is foaming at the mouth now. I've winked at his lady, ran a wheel on him with his lady while being her partner, and now I'm talking shit on top of it. I probably ought to stop it, because it's probably going to cause a domestic disturbance tonight after the lockdown. Once again, I'm just being who I'm supposed to be.

So, they deal out the cards for the first hand of the second game, and it doesn't work out as good as the last hand, but we do make eight books. The dominant of the two is now trying to exert his power over the poor little fish by intimidating him into bidding for more books than he has. This is unacceptable, because I ain't trying to get set and I ain't gonna let my he/she partner lose the game of spades for me. "Just bid your hand baby girl." I tell her in a calm reassuring voice, and she does. We go on to make seven books that hand. Now the score is fifteen to twelve our way and the race is to thirty-five. Next hand, we get nine which is really pissing the husband off. See, no one suspects this guy is pounding or getting pounded by the lady boy in this unit, except for me. I wouldn't have had he been able to control his emotions throughout my psychological fuckeries at the card table. This makes the game about so much more than playing cards.

I'm playing with emotions. It can be dangerous, but I needed to pass the time, remember? We make our nine, and now have twenty-four to their sixteen, and ole' boy is pissed. I promise you it's always the super competitive, most homophobic, quickest to get in a fight sons a bitches who get caught in the shower with a shaft in their ass, and this is no different, which is why I'm basking in his rage. Maybe it's wrong, but don't feel like it. So, I keep on keeping on until we finally win. Two games are enough for me, so I excuse myself from the table, leaving them talking shit and punching the lady boy in the arms simultaneously. It looks like brotherly love or spousal abuse, don't really matter to me which one it is.

Now it's lunch time. It don't really matter what it is, because if someone is hungry anything tastes good, and being that my box is empty, I'll be eating anything they put on my tray. Just like the old Proverb says, "to a hungry soul, even what's bitter tastes sweet." It's very true in reality. pasta noodles, chopped up turkey meat, cubed carrots, three duplex cookies and a piece of white bread. Oh, and a grape juice pack, is what lunch consists of. Even so, I say my thanks, sprinkle some chili noodle seasoning on it and tear that shit up.

It's still only ten in the morning, lunch is over with, and all that's left to look forward to is dinner. Our existence revolves around feeding time. It's what we look forward to, and what we do our time around. "Three meals" is a day and then three more is another. All we have to do is wait in line to get them. Time rolls on. There is nothing for me to do so I opt to hop on my wheel and do some walking.

As I walk around and around, stopping occasionally to view the tv, I look at all my fellow inmates. Most are straining their neck, and seem to be in a trance like state watching TV. Others are playing cards, dominoes, or chess. Then you have groups in cells having tea parties or the like. For most, jail is a complete waste of time. Which more than not makes men worse not better. The sad part of that is the government tries to claim they are helping, or rehabilitating us, which is complete and utter bullshit, just like everything else the government claims. Think about just this one thing or two really, then I'll get back to us doing time. The Department of Defense is always on the attack, which completely contradicts its name. The Department of Justice will allow someone guilty to go free if they have enough money and will let you commit crimes as long as you rat on others, which is completely unjust. You love your government, ain't that sweet. I guess love truly is blind. Back to the story though.

My fellow inmates, I believe, were people in a deep hypnotic state while watching some bullshit on tv. I'd rather leave those zombies alone, so I try and find myself a tea party, to attend, uninvited of course. I walk in the lady boy and macho man's room to find them both sitting on the bottom bunk with the macho man's feet in the lady boy's lap. This confirms my suspicions or doubts I may have had. The way I see it, as long as it's consensual, and both parties are happy, it's their business. I'm no judge, my philosophy and sincere belief in freedom won't allow me to hinder them in their actions as long as they aren't harming anyone. Apparently, they are ok with it. So, it's their business. Anyhow, I stay and visit these two for a second, and then think to myself, "What would these walls say if they could talk?" My mind starts heading down the path of destruction, and I quickly slam that door before I throw-up a perfectly good lunch. The shame is screaming at me from the walls and both of their eyes. So, I bid them farewell and go in search of another type of tea party.

Right after exiting the lovers lounge, I smell smoke and I'm off to investigate. It doesn't smell like tobacco or weed. But it is definitely smoke, and it doesn't take me long to zero in on where it was coming from or what it was being used for. They are burning ink upstairs, obviously making preparation for some jailhouse tats. Fun fact: face tattoos are free here. Even if you don't have any commissary or a hustle you can at least get your face tattooed. This is one of the few things given away out of pure hurt and brotherly love. I'm curious, and have nothing but time on my hands, so I head upstairs to join in on the madness.

Sure enough, top tier, last cell on the walk. They made a candle out of a bar of soap hollowed out with a wick made from twisted toilet paper and petroleum jelly as the fuel source. It's a very simple setup. You just build yourself a candle and then set it under something to collect the soot. Once the soot has built up and looks like an ant bed turned upside down, you gently scrape it off, put it into a bag or small bottle, add a drop or two of alcohol. If you can't get an alcohol pad add a couple slivers of clear deodorant, and a couple of drops of water and you've got yourself some ink.

That's what I've just walked into. They've got their candle inside the built in toilet paper slot of the stainless-steel toilet. (It's a sink and toilet paper holder combo.) The only problem with what these geniuses have going on is the fact that they didn't use a piece of paper and toothpaste to make a flu, which controls air flow and also keeps the valuable soot from escaping. This is also the reason I was able to smell their actions. If done properly, the guys in the cell next to you wouldn't even smell what you had going on. Being that I don't feel like getting shook down and showing a stranger my private parts, I step in and help these rookies out. I'm all about jailhouse tats and not getting caught. Once again, I play my part.

Bad really is good. Just as I thought time couldn't slow down anymore, I get blessed with a whole plateful of activities to choose from. I bet you never knew there could be so much to do. Maybe by now you know why we keep coming back. It's not that it's a trap and the entire system is designed to keep the social order in effect. It's the fact that we have so much fun here. We practically break our way into prison. I had a judge tell me that one time. I thought I was minding my own business and trying to stay out of the way, but he thought otherwise. It was also strange that he thought that. They swarmed my house to get me and forcefully took me to jail instead of me climbing the fence and sneaking in the backdoor. Hell, I'm the crazy one though, so what he said must have been true. Although I can't quite remember how I broke in, because if I could, I promise you, I would use that same method to break out. Aha! It just hit me; he must be meaning the exact opposite just like the government he represents. They let boys claim to be girls and vice versa. By him saying I appear to be trying to break into jail, he really meant that I was doing my best to stay out, but I'm caught in a web of lies, deceit, and evil. Now I get it. Everything said is really the exact opposite. I'm finally catching on.

Back to the business. We've got paper covering most of the hole now. The soot is no longer escaping, and we've got one on damage control with a soap sock downstairs. Nothing left to do now except hurry up and wait, and while we do that I ask, "Pick poke or ya'll got a gun?" He replies, "Just pick poke bro. I wish we had a gun." I nod and say, "as do I friend. As do I." I'm way past the point in my career where I get pick poke tattoos. They take too long, come out like shit, and you just have to get them done over again once you get around someone with a gun. I suppose they do take up time, and that's what this is all about, right?

The candle burns out, and now is the moment of truth. Time to find out if all the efforts have been fruitless or if they will have what they need to put some tear drops under one another's eyes. And there it is, a small, inverted cone of soot directly above where the flame was burning. Just enough to keep two young men from landing a decent job and to help ruin their lives forever. Today is turning out to be a good day. Thank God we don't live in a society that bases almost everything on looks or worldly possessions, and one that doesn't hold a man's past against him. We would be fucked if that's how our society truly worked. Just as I'm thinking this, I look at the tattoo on my left hand that says, "Once guilty, never forgiven" And realize that the society I just thought about is exactly the one we live in. At least I'm not the only one that is fucked.

Now that the soot is collected and being mixed, I take a glance at what they've rigged up as their pic pokes. They've taken two staples out of a writing pad, two "State Issued" toothbrushes, and cling wrap then bent the staples into the shape of an L, put the little part of the L into a hole that once held toothbrush bristles and wrapped it real tight with cling wrap. After securing the staples they sharpen it on the wall and are ready to begin. You may be concerned about sanitation, but I promise you it's going to take a hell of a lot more than this to kill you. Looks like they are all ready, and I ask, "are you two going to do each other at the same time?" They say, "Hell Naw!" quickly, and we get a laugh out of it.

I show them how to take the cap off some state issued toothpaste, put some Vaseline in it with your finger leaving an impression, and then put a couple of drops of ink in and you're ready to go. If they catch you getting tattoos they charge you with self-mutilation, which once again makes absolutely no motherfucking sense. It's beautification in our eyes, but what we believe is irrelevant. I almost forgot my place in society and the world. I must have been thinking we were free.

Next, they draw their teardrops on with a pen, both ask me if I think they look good, and I confer. Then it begins the ancient tradition of tattooing. This is far from what happens in tattoo shops as no one is wearing gloves, ain't shit disinfected, and they definitely ain't professionals. Anyway, they both end up bleeding with black teardrops under their eyes. I've already got mine so after watching them defile the holy temple of their body, I make my way back out into the neighborhood to see what else I can find to entertain my mind.

I have almost forgotten about all the shit I brought with me from the last jail, but as soon as I think about it, I know it's a lost cause. A mouth will say anything, and me arguing with these people over that will do nothing except get my blood pressure up, and slow my time down. I put that thought out of my mind, and settled on walking a couple of laps. I'll eventually start doing pushups and squats along with my walking, but my heart just ain't in it right now. I mean fuck, I got three and a half years to do what'll only take me six months. So that can wait. Besides, I did all that on my last bid and you know what those wash boards abs got me when I got out on parole? A treacherous bitch! That's what they got me, and I'm trying to never land one of those again as long as I live. Besides, I'm on a mission to come up with the right words to wake up those who are asleep. Hopefully, I'll leave the world a better place than what I found it. If I can't do that, I need to get rich, buy a boat, and get the fuck out of ya'll's way.

Midway through a lap around the unit, I hear the door unlock and a guard comes in and calls my celly out. I'm not sure what he's got going on, but I'm sure I'll find out shortly. So, I just keep on keeping on, just a walking along steadily, moving but going nowhere, and then I decide to take a nap. Enough is enough, and I'm exhausted. So, I head to my cell, take a piss, then crawl in my bunk to hopefully sleep until sandwich bags comes at five. That doesn't happen, because as soon as my celly comes back from wherever he went, he wakes me up. This is unusual, but being just awakened from my slumber, I don't realize it and immediately jump off the rack and on my feet in case a riot or banging has jumped off. "Take it easy bro," he says.

I'm like, "Hell man, I ain't used to being woke up. What's up?"

"I've got some shit to tell you, but I'm gonna wait till tonight after we lock down. That's what they told me to do."

I look at him like "what the fuck dude?" I don't press him. I know he just went out and spoke with someone, and I don't doubt they told him to tell me something that they can't tell me themselves. So once again I try to remain patient, now having lockdown to look forward to. I bet you never thought someone could look forward to being locked into a cell, have you?

I swear, just as soon as things speed up something comes to slow them down. My mind is now going crazy with different thoughts about what my celly has to say and why he must wait until night after lockdown. This and that, it's just the bullshit that life works sometimes. I thought time was moving slow, now this shit. I tell you one thing, if I do turn out to be crazy, the fucking system drove me that way. Believe that!

Finally sandwich bag comes and I really am hungry, so I eat right after they pass them out. I don't do any trading. For some reason today has just been sort of gloomy, not sure if it's because I finally signed the plea or if it's just one of them days. I can tell you this, I'm ready for it to end and tomorrow to begin. I know that we are only granted so many days, and everyone lives his own, but some are better than others, and some just need to end in order for another to begin.

Another bullshit ass meal down, and I'm none the better for it. As always, I'm thankful, and therefore give my God thanks for a meal that sustains my life. Then it's back to my hamster wheel, and round and round I go, where I'll stop is not hard to know. As I make my way past the cells, I'm overwhelmed with the smell of cocoa butter. I can't quite pinpoint exactly where the smell is coming from, because I was moving kind of fast and wasn't quite suspecting that sweet smelling aroma. I make sure to slow down on my next lap and narrow the smell down to two cells. It's either the lady boy's or the one next to it. I do catch an underlying scent of something else mixed with the cocoa butter, but I can't quite make it out. You see how even the smallest things are so significant to an idle mind? That's why it's crucial to think positive thoughts; once evil takes root, some are never able to pull it out.

The next lap I noticed something very strange. One of the cell doors was all the way closed. We still have three hours until lockdown time, and now I'm suspicious. The wheels are turning round and round in my mind and my feet keep carrying me in the same direction. The next pass, by the wall with the cells, and I've no doubt where the sweet smell is coming from, and I catch a faint hint of something else. The two smells seem combined with the cocoa being sweet while the whatever is blended with it, almost has a rancid and raunchy quality about it. This shit got me puzzled: no one uses cocoa butter to cover up the smell of shit. Now I know. Now I stop walking, now I stop talking, or better yet writing about the forbidden. Now my nose is running, and I've got extra saliva in my mouth that comes before you throw up.

Now I really need some fresh air, but I can't get any. Now I've smelt that which can't be unsmelt and I'm none the better for it. Now I must go lie down.

My head is spinning, my stomach is soured, and my life may forever be charged by the smell of prison love. I hope you never have to smell such a thing. It can ruin your appetite and possibly even your soul. There is no way in hell I could be a part of such a thing as this, and I pity anyone caught in the snares. These are the thoughts running through my mind as sleep overtakes me. All I know is, I hope I don't have nightmares behind this shit.

6 God is Good

The cell door slamming shut awakens me and signifies its ten o'clock at night. I was fortunate enough to sleep until lockdown, without dreams of gay porn, and now it's time to see what my cell mate has to say. What could've been so important it had to wait until lockdown, when anything we say can be heard by the guards? There is an intercom in every cell and it's used as a one-way listening device. I proved this point years ago by telling my cellmate I was going to light a bible on fire and throw it out our tray flap at the preacher and see how he would react. Of course, I was just talking shit and wouldn't do such a thing, but those listening didn't know that. Thirty-seconds after the words came out of my mouth, the door to the pod buzzed and in came two guards on a beeline directly to my cell. They buzzed my door open, took a quick peak inside, shined their flashlight in my eyes, and I said, "I was just talking shit." They slammed my cell door shut and walked out of the unit, all the while the preacher was steadily preaching and trying to figure out what the hell we had going on. So, the point is, they are always listening.

The door is shut, the lights are out, and the walls are listening when I ask my celly, "What's up bro? What's so important we had to wait until tonight for you to tell me?" He looks at me and says, "You know I went out today, right?" I'm committed to knowing what everyone else knows and says, "of course, I know motherfucker, what do you have to say? Why are you dragging this shit out?" I guess he didn't want me to think he'd been talking to the police, but I couldn't give two fucks who he had been talking to, or telling on or whatever. After reassuring him he is in no danger, he says, "They were asking me about you, and they wanted me to tell you something." I feel anger start to rise in me, and my heartbeat accelerates. This is not good; I need to stay in control and not pummel this fool for talking to the cops about me. This fucking son of bitch had me thinking he was my friend, but in reality, he has been saying God knows what about me to the people who put me in here. I gave him my word though, so I get my emotions under control and ask him, "What did they have to say?"

I almost don't believe what he tells me. It's the shit you hear about. This is the shit movies are made of, it's something people on my side of the fence dream of and something we all wish to attain. They said to tell you, "When this is all over, and you do, whatever time you have to do, you can do what you do and as long as you work, don't have the neighbors suspicious, and never fuck with them again. They won't fuck with you." End quote. Believe it or not, this is the god damn truth. I mean, in this fictional book it's the truth. I'll leave the decision up to you all. I know it's what my celly told me.

I don't say anything when he tells me this. I just kinda looked at him and thought about the weight of the words he just told me. Now I know why he had to wait until lockdown, and we were in our cell. They wanted to listen in on the conversation, and no doubt hear my reaction. I'm not sure exactly how I feel about what he just told me or even speaking on it just yet. Sometimes it's best to remain silent. To control the tongue is a great strength. It's easier said than done, but once you gain control over it, you damn near control your destiny.

"So, what do you think about that bro?" He asked me.

"I'm still thinking on it. I'll have to let you know sometime in the near future", I reply. I then he is like, "Fuck, I wish they would tell me that." I look at the poor fool and say, "I bet you do."

Me on the other hand, I know this runs much deeper than getting high or having guns or any shit like that. To be told something like that when I haven't done anything for them makes me question it. I could understand them letting their informants get by like that, but I haven't informed them of anything. Perhaps a change is coming, although they may not be able to speak of it, maybe, just maybe, it is creeping into the hearts and minds of men. Maybe that's my purpose to say or write what others can't say or write, but inwardly believe. Aint' that about a bitch? And then that age old enemy, doubt, starts to creep into my mind. from its dark crevices and hiding places. I doubt the validity of his words. It could all be a lie. I don't know what he would gain from such. If there is no gain, what would another ulterior motive be? Then my wits try and make a comeback. I almost forgot what I know. You can't understand someone who doesn't understand themselves. I've no doubt this man is lacking in his own understanding. That pretty much rules out him fabricating this whole story. He stands to gain nothing or anything higher than getting out or bodily profit is too high for him in his current state of mind. So, my reasoning skills fight off my doubt and once again, I believe what he just told me. Fuck my life!

This shit just got deeper, and here I am. Talk about a double-edged sword. They just gave me free reign, which I believe we all should have, but I don't know the price that I must pay, or have already paid, for it. Perhaps it's to keep quiet and keep my thoughts to myself. Well, that's obviously not going to happen as my God has beat them to the punch on that. It's no use running from God. Maybe though they see the whole situation, and maybe they feel as if I've paid enough already. Just the thought of that makes me want to cry, jump for joy, and start the revolution. I know if they can understand me just as I understand them, then God has touched their lives just as mine has been touched. If this is the case, the task no longer seems so daunting. If it's really true, then those I once thought were enemies, have just become my allies. If that be the case, God is good. In fact, when I finally do reply to my cellmate that's exactly what I say, "God is good." And all he says in return is, "Yes He is."

After that we both hop in our bunks to sleep, or think, or anything besides talk more. Small talk would be unfitting, and everything else just really doesn't matter at the moment. Luckily, just as always, once I close my eyes and think of nothing, I fall asleep.

The door buzzes, and I hear, "Sleep late, lose weight" so I hop out of my bunk and make my way into the feeding line. A guy coming down the stairs says, "Good morning everybody." Some people reply, but I don't. He says the same shit every morning, and it's more about tradition than actually giving a fuck about whether it's a good morning or not. Him and his whole good morning shit reminds me of the old proverb that says, "he who greets his neighbor loudly in the morning will be counted as a curse instead of a blessing." That shoe definitely fits in this situation because its six in the god damn morning and people just want to get their food, eat, and then go back to sleep. Hopefully, no one pushes him down the stairs behind that good morning bullshit, or better yet, hopefully he gets whatever the Good Lord deems fit.

Breakfast goes off without a hitch, and before long I'm back in my bunk full as a tic and tossing and turning, trying to get comfortable enough to dose back off. I know I ate too much, but I guess it's comfort eating. Maybe I'm trying to reach that thanksgiving day full when you eat so much you pass into a food induced coma and wake up several hours later lightheaded, still full, but wanting more food and needing to take a shit all at the same time. God damn our views and flaws to say the least. I'm starting to think I am crazy, then that sweet sleep takes over me.

7 Judgement Day

I hear my name and jump up immediately to see what's going on. After opening my door, I look out across an empty zone, only to find a CO standing at the door. He looks at me and says, "you've got court, get ready." This is a surprise blessing. I figured it would be weeks, but apparently my lawyer knew which strings to pull, and did, on my behalf. I'm certainly in debt now, which I don't mind being, because as I said earlier, she and I are on the same side. But anyways I brushed my teeth and then rubbed my hair and beard every which way to give myself that unkept disheveled look that inmates are supposed to have, and make my way out after taking a piss. Hopefully, my looks, and the dark circles of misery around my eyes will be enough to convince the judge to accept the plea and have a little mercy on me.

Down the hall, around the bend, through booking, and into the van. Then the wheels on the van go round and round, round, and round. The wheels on the van take us right downtown, right, downtown. The wheels on the van stopped at the courthouse steps. The door opens, I almost fall on my face because of the shackles, but gain my composure and walk up the steps to once again be judged for my actions. Fuck my life!

Up the steps, through the doors, take a left up more steps, take a right through a doorway, and into the prison holding room behind the judge's chambers. I took a seat on the makeshift benches some county employees who were far from a furniture maker made. They are too high, and not nearly wide enough. The window has been covered with a piece of plywood and painted the same color as the sheetrock, and the sheetrock walls have gang graffiti scratched into them as high as a pair of shackled hands can reach. Hopefully, that paints the picture for you. So here I sit and here I wait.

I'd like to tell you that I'm nervous or that time tries to pull some bullshit on me, but that would be a lie. I'm not going to tell you that. All I can tell you is that once again a man, or a system made up of men and women, is about to sentence me to prison. I haven't harmed a single soul. Perhaps fate guided me to this point to be able to express my feelings to you. The good sheeple of the world. Perhaps fate had nothing to do with it, and I'm simply a criminal who knows how to organize words into sentences that have no meaning. Perhaps I'm completely nuts, but a decent English student. I'll let you decide on that.

After sitting here for I don't know how long, my lawyer opens the door and pops her welcoming, warm, but at the same time worn face into the room. She asks, "You all ready? Any questions?" I shake my head and say, "No ma'am." She gives me a quick knowing nod before she leaves. I say, "Thank you." She replies with her eyes, and shuts the door. Now I just have to await my turn.

Although our perception of time may speed up or slow down, one thing I've yet to experience is it stopping. Before I know it, it's my time. They opened the door to the holding cell. They lead me to the right, down a very narrow hallway, and then to the left to emerge into the courtroom from behind the judge, and to his right. A quick glance around reveals my mother, who would have been there even if she had to tread water, then walk on coal to make it. She would have been on time as well, which is a trait she instilled in me. I also see the prosecutor, my attorney, several bailiffs. members of the Sheriff's Department, and two others, soon to be convicts. Talk about feeling like just another number. The three of us are all lined up together, and go through the whole process from answering questions to prove our competency, all the way to pleading guilty to our crimes together. The courts are so wise they figured out a way to get three in the same amount of time it should take one. If anyone ever thought highly of themselves, they have never been in a position such as this. Just another sheep headed for the slaughter. The only difference between us and the sheep is we know what's coming, and they don't.

After answering, "Yes, Sir and no Sir" to all the questions, the judge read our charges individually. He then reads the plea bargains we've all struck with the government. Generally, you can get a lesser sentence by admitting your guilt and not forcing the government to take you to trial. The catch is that the judge has the power to accept the terms of the plea or to pass his own sentence to you. Being that you just admitted guilt there ain't no backing out, so you are fucked if his or her majesty wants to give you more than the plea deal. The good thing is that the system is so corrupt by backroom deals and favors owed for favors accepted, that as long as you are in someone's good graces you've got a chance to cheat an unjust justice system. Now it's time to make sure I haven't pissed the wrong one off.

My testicles are on the block and its nut cutting time. As the judge listens to the prosecutor present my plea. He reads of a thirteen-year sentence with five on probation and eight to serve, but then by the grace of God says, "The Sheriff's

Department has recommended suspending this sentence as long as the defendant completes two years in a trustee program here at the county jail." The judge accepts because no one wants to piss off the Sheriff's Department. Just like that, I escaped being made a eunuch. I believe I'll name my next son after the sheriff. The conversation last night in my cell also makes a hell of a lot more sense now. The plan is coming together.

Then, just as fast as it started, it's over. I send a thank you upstairs, shake my lawyer's hand, and tell her the same before being led back through the corridors, down the stairs and into the awaiting Patty wagon. Just as they close the doors one of the bailiffs who was a correctional officer on my last bid ask me in a friendly manner, "When are you going to get your act together?" I just give him a sly grin and say, "hopefully this time." The door shuts, and we are off to the county jail from which I came.

His words leave me pondering on my life and my beliefs. Perhaps I am just a rebellious motherfucker, but perhaps it's a curse to have higher ideas. Am I the only one who believes it's OK to do what you do as long as you don't hurt anyone while doing it? Ain't no way I'm the only one. All these men on the same side of the fence as me believe the same, but we are obviously not the ones in power. I believe those in power believe the same, but the world we inherited and the system in the place, is far from the ideology. If that system is run by words on paper, those words are the true enemy. And how do you fight words? Well with twords of course. I need that commissary to come so I can have that pen and paper. My weapons and ammunition!

8 Hell into Heaven

Now that I know my fate, I must remain patient. Now that I've been sentenced to be a trustee, I'll be leaving the pretrial county jail side and moving on up into the trustee zone. It's still incarceration, but if there can be such a thing as "good time" this will be it. Just imagine going from a place where you are fortunate to have a cup, bowl, an extra blanket, to a place where you can't even have a real pen. I'm coming from a place where you must use a flex pen, which is a real piece of shit, drink out of a sink connected to the toilet, get your coffee water and cooking water out of the same sink, with no contraband whatsoever; to a place with couches, a microwave, cigarettes, a fridge, and a door that opens at 6:00 AM and locks at 10:00 PM. These things may seem frivolous or trivial to you, but here it's the small things that count. Back to the point though. Even though I'm sentenced, it could be a day, an hour, or even a motherfucking month, until I get moved from this hell hole to the other side. The last thing I want is for my patience to wear thin and lose my shit when the light is right around the corner.

I tried my hand with the lady in booking, saying, "I just got sentenced to the trustee side. Could you please go ahead and move me in the computer?" As you might have imagined, my words fall on deaf ears and she replies, "Oh no. I can't do that until your paperwork arrives from the court." What can I say, I had to try. If you remember, this is the same lady that didn't want to go through my property when I arrived from the other jail. I knew my chances were slim to none, but how would I know it if I didn't try? I've been told "no" plenty of times, and although it used to be disheartening, after so much time it builds up calluses. I tried, and I failed, so now I'm headed back to my old cell and my old celly to wait.

Wait and wait and wait some more, and then I realized I missed lunch. A closed mouth don't get fed. I get on the intercom with the tower and prepare myself for yet another battle, but to my surprise, once I plead my case with the lady on the other side of the intercom, she tells me a CO is on the way with my tray. I want it to be a lie. Well, I don't really want it to be, but let's say I expect it to be. I head into my cell telling myself that in five minutes I'll get back on the horn and try it again.

Once again, for far too many times to be normal, I hear the door pop open, and there stands a guard with my food. This shit is really starting to trip me the fuck out. Things are going too smoothly. Pieces are falling into place, and either I'm doing exactly what I'm supposed to be doing, or the universe is setting me up for a fall. I certainly hope it's not the fall, because falls I've had too many of. At this point, I don't know if I can handle another one.

I make my way out, and grab the food, all the while looking up and expecting a lightning strike or even a light fixture to fall on my head. Neither happens, and as always, I say thanks and eat my food without tasting it. Then, later than should have been, the bombardment starts from my fellow inmates. I tell them everything that happened at court no less than eight times. I'm congratulated by some, while others excuse themselves from the conversation, obviously hating. That's on them, let the haters hate. Gossip hour finally dies down and it's finally just me and my celly in the cell. I wonder how that would go over in the toy world. Every kid could have his own, "My Celly," complete with prison ink and a detachable shank. It would probably be a bestseller considering how many children's fathers are locked up in the land of the free.

Funny, but not funny. There is no substitute for a father and that is one of the root problems in this country. How to fix it is still above me, but recognizing the problem is the first step to fixing it. I know in my case, it's either to change my sincerely held beliefs on freedom, or open the eyes of the world to what freedom truly is. Once again, I need that pad and pen.

My cellmate gets my thoughts out of the clouds, and congratulates me on my success at court. He is a genuine and sincere person that means what he says. I feel somewhat bad for doubting what he told me last night or even suspecting him of ulterior motives. He just got caught up in some shit above his head and was just the messenger. "Now what they told you yesterday makes a little more sense don't it, cuz." I told him. He gives me a grave look, and nods in agreement. "So, the law does have a conscience." I go on further to say.

He says, "you ain't no bad dude man, and they know that. They know that bitch shot you through a cross." I don't really want to get into that. I already got thrown in the hole for writing her a letter forgiving her, but also telling her to seek forgiveness from God, because, "vengeance is mine saith the Lord, and I will repay." I've left that in hands much stronger than mine, and must move on and play the hand I've been dealt.

So, we decide to have us a cup of lukewarm coffee from our, all-in-one shitter and sink combo, and wait. And wait, we do. In the meantime, we exchange information because we know our time is drawing to an end. Contrary to popular belief there are some real good guys in here. Guys that give when they don't have to give. Men who care and try and uplift others when they see they are down. Guys who have a heart. That's what everyone needs to understand. It doesn't matter what clothes someone has on, or their job title their religion, or virtues or vices, skin color, or lineage, good and bad exist in all of these. Good priest and child molesting priests; good cops and bad cops just judges and unjust judges, us, and even good cons and bad cons. Good and bad is in all of us and it's a battle we all must wage. This is why we must look deeper into someone than what they wear, where they live, their creeds or customs, and learn to see the soul of a person. The ability is in all of us. We've just never been told we have the power to do such things. Believe in the unbelievable, because it's true. Let your heart judge a person. We all know that gut feeling we have, no one denies it, but we've learned to ignore it because of what our eyes and ears tell us. If we all did this the world would change instantly, and just as this one man inspired me to write this, we would all inspire one another to be who we were made to be, and live in a world that is the way it's supposed to be.

Ask yourself this question, "do I need to be told what to do?" Now I'm not talking about the first day of a new job. I'm talking about right and wrong. I've yet to meet a motherfucker who doesn't know right from wrong. Once again, I'm not talking about what you've been told. I could care less about that. I'm asking you what does your "you" say is right and wrong? My "me" says right is whatever you want it to be, as long as it doesn't hurt life without reason.

My God gave me free will and the ability to decide my right and wrong, and that's what I came up with. I'm not here to judge your conscience, and you're not here to judge mine. That is between me and the creator. Where we went astray is when man hungered for power, sought, and found it, and then to keep their firm grasp on it, imposed their will on others. This is not good, and has gotten far out of control. They view us as fools with no mind, no heart, no soul, just mere subjects at their disposal. They are wrong because the same creator created us all, and did not intend for one to rule over another. We are all people with different gifts, but we are not supposed to be used or abused, lied to, or done wrong. God sees all man. it's time all men started to see all as well.

And just like, that it's time for Bologna sandwiches, my favorite, not really, but it makes me feel better about the situation. I was hoping to get moved, but once again I'm strengthening my patience, which is a truly hard virtue for me to attain, but nonetheless it's being forced upon me. I really don't have a say in the present matter, so I chew, and swallow, without even adding the mustard to the sandwiches. The shit wouldn't help much anyway. Then it happens the gates are swung open, the light shines through the dark, they call my name and tell me to pack my shit.

Six months to the day since my initial arrest, and the sentencing is all over. I'm finally going to start doing my time. Fuck the cookies and baby carrots. I'm not even sure what I did with them. I'm packing my shit, while simultaneously fending off the vultures and shaking hands with friends. The damn buzzards know I'm just moving to the other side, and will therefore be able to take all my belongings, which only consists of: a mat, two blankets, a fork, boxers, socks and a plastic cup and bowl. I mean god damn, just when I want to love them and think better of them, I have to deal with this bullshit. Then, just as I can feel the anger rising inside of me, I remind myself that they are seeing with their eyes, instead of their hearts, and I'm able to keep my composure.

I say my goodbyes, and just as I'm about to walk out of the unit, my celly runs up and hands me a piece of paper with this information written on it. We shake hands and the door slams behind me. As I walk away you may think it's all joy that I'm feeling at the moment, but you will be incorrect. I feel for the ones I'm leaving behind. Well, I feel for most of them. My joyous moments are mixed with sorrow. I've made it out, but they are still in. Mind you, I'm not all the way out, but I'm out of the worst of it. They are still trapped. Who would have known there could be so many different worlds within our world?

There are. If you didn't know, now you do. You can count it as a blessing and a curse. Blessed, if your life has been constant with God's protecting hedge all around you, but also cursed with blindness by not seeing what others all around you may be or are going through. I've been cursed with having it all and then having nothing. Cursed with being in God's favor, and then falling from grace. Through it all, I've come out blessed by knowing how someone on both sides feels, blessed with being able to understand why someone did what they did, or who they are. I guess at the end of the day I had to go through what I went through in order to be who I am. And I am who I am, and I'm completely content with that.

God damn it's a long walk to where I'm going. After

doing not much of nothing for the past six months, this mat is heavy, and just when I'm about to say, "Fuck it" , and start dragging it, we arrive back in booking. I drop my shit by the door and head to the dressing room to get my used but new to me, bright orange trustee uniform. "Thank God, clothes don't make the man!

"What size you wear?" the storage asked me.

"Large or extra-large."

He looks me up and down and says, "Hell naw! Two-X."

Once again, not a battle worth fighting. So, I put the shirt on. I know once I get in the back, I can just pay the laundry guy some noodles or cigarettes and he will bring me the sizes I need. Wisdom. So, then he asked, "what kind of shoes you have in your property?"

I told him, "I've got some two strap institutional Jays in the bag of shit I brought from the other jail."

He disappears into the property room, and I'm left alone with the Major over the jail.

The major is a good man. I know one when I see one. He looks me square in the eyes and says, "You're fortunate to get this program. Don't fuck it up, because your balls are in my hands." I wanted to laugh, but the moment was far too serious. He likes me, and I'm sure he played a crucial role in pulling the right strings to get me here. We all walk out and now I'm really catching hell trying to carry all this shit and after what seemed like half a mile, I'm once again ready to start dragging some of this shit, and kicking the rest. When I thought I couldn't go no more, we arrive, the door unlocks, and all the officers escorted me in. I respect his position, and the fact that he has to tell me this shit, because it comes with the territory. It would have been funny as hell though to tell him he could cup my balls with just one hand because they aren't that big. But it wasn't the right time, plus I sincerely appreciated him for allowing me into this "trustee program." Therefore, I say, "I really appreciate it," and "I thank you for all you've done." You won't have a problem out of me. I don't think I told him anything he didn't already know. He gives me a nod just as the sarge is entering the dressing room with my laundry bag full of belongings and the shoes I was wearing that fateful day that the shit hit the fan.

I enter into the closest thing I've known to heaven in a long time. Jesus said the Kingdom of heaven is within you, and I can relate to that. But your surroundings play a major role in what's within you. If heaven is happiness, joy, love and all the other good shit, how can our surroundings not play a crucial role in all the feelings inside of us? Just like the soul is connected to the body, we are connected to our surroundings. Here my surroundings are better, so I feel better.

They escort me to my rack, and bid me farewell. This zone is an open bay, 50-man zone, with only seven of us in here, including myself. There is a fridge, microwave, air fryer, and toaster oven. They may seem insignificant to you, but as I've said, something is better than nothing. This is a whole lot of something for anywhere behind razor wire and chain link fences, lock doors and community showers. If you've got to do it, this is the place to do it. Unfortunately, I've got to do it, so here I am. After throwing my mat on the bunk and dropping the laundry bag, the major is bombarded with questions and requests from other guys in the zone. I slide my way to the kiosk and try to log in so I can send my mother a message informing her of my move. I know she will be just as ecstatic as I am, and for that I love her all the more.

Speaking of my mother, one couldn't say enough. She is there no matter what, fills in where I left off with my kids, and was once blind, but now sees full well the meaning of justice in America. Before I started my career as a bad guy, she assumed, like most, that the law, the courts, the whole system, was the way TV shows portrayed it. It's sad to say, but my life and decisions have cost the both of us, yet at the same time we were both blessed with a fairly good idea of how shit really works. I wouldn't trade what I know and have learned for all the money in the world. Now she may not quite agree with that at the moment, but that's just because of the current circumstances. When things get better, and this is a memory, she will agree. Remember what the Bible says, "wisdom, knowledge, and understanding are worth more than all the silver and gold in the world." Just think about it, with those attributes, gaining silver and gold is a small feat.

Unfortunately, they haven't moved me in the system yet, so I can't log in or send the message. So what do I opt for next? A motherfucking cigarette! And it just so happens that I happen to have some, which is a blessing because that means I don't have to "two for one" myself one. Then I realized, the folks are still in here, so that means I'm going to have to wait. Patience once again I swear, when it's your time to learn something in life, every event seems to center around teaching you that virtue.

If you're wondering why I must wait until the people leave, your memory is failing you, or you're not paying attention. My tobacco is in the bottom of peanut butter jars, and the last thing I want the officers to see or know is that I had what would have been contraband at the time; tobacco hidden inside the peanut butter. Two reasons for this are they blessed me with the trustee shit, and I don't want them to catch on to the play and ruin it for someone in the future. They would have probably frowned at the fact that I was, and actually did, introduce some contraband into the facility. In my defense I don't think it's wrong, against the rules perhaps, but not wrong. It's my job to do such things. There is no monetary gain, just a mere mental kick in the nuts to assist those who violate the whole population on a daily basis.

Patience is a virtue, and I need all the help I can get. I remain patient until the guards and convicts finish their conversations and eventually leave. Now I proceed with the business at hand, scooping the peanut butter out, washing off the bags, remove the outer bag, then the next bag. I then find out that the brown is not contaminated with peanut butter. I put the peanut butter back in the jar, and I tear off a piece of Bible paper and roll myself a cigarette. Now I know what you're thinking, about me smoking Bible paper, but the way I see it is this; The Lord will provide, so whether I need to gain inspiration, knowledge, wisdom, understanding, or a rolling paper, God has got me covered with the Bible. They also serve as great smuggling devices and address books. God really knows how to kill seven birds with one stone.

Smoking isn't permitted inside here, so I head out the back door (which opens at 5:00 AM and closes at 10:00 PM) to the yard to catch a light from someone. It's going down out here. These fools are smoking joints, hitting the weights playing basketball, and talking shit. To each his own, I ain't smoking no weed, cause there's time and place for everything, and right now, right here, don't seem like the right time for all that. I do get a light and meet all the guys by the weight pile. The cigarette is as good as I thought it would be. I suck at name remembering, so I don't remember anyone's name as I leave and head back inside the unit.

Back inside, and back to business. I make the bed, find an empty locker, put all my shit in order, send that message to mom, and then lay back and chill. I came to realize I haven't sent a thanks upstairs for this move, and I do so. I should have done it sooner, but it's better late than never.

9 Just Another Day in Paradise

For some reason we all eat four meals a day on this side. There are the three bullshit meals they serve us, and at night another. I like to call these nightly meals "penitentiary plates", and they range from a simple noodle to a pizza made from tortillas to deep fried burritos (fried with lard in a garbage with a strainer dropped inside), to honey bun with peanut butter on it. All have their time and place. Tonight, I'm keeping it simple, with chilly noodles and a mackerel pack topped with hot sauce flavored pork skins. Well, when I started that sentence, it was going to be simple. Now, I just kept thinking, and writing, and decided not to stop at noodle. Since today has been a good day, I'm going to celebrate with a nice meal.

There's only one microwave, so at dinner time the poor device gets a major workout. You are in and out, cooking things separately. You then wait while the next man or group of men get in and out. As long as everyone remains courteous it flows pretty well. So, it's me cooking my little feast, and a group of guys cooking a meal together. Really, it's one guy cooking for three. Only two of us are using the microwave. What they got going on is common; it's usually a friend who doesn't make canteen cooking for his buddies. I'm new, but fitting in easily and quickly, plus I like talking shit. So, the man cooking and myself are shit talking when his buddies ask me, "Sir, could you please stop fraternizing with the help? We are hungry." Now I know they are just talking shit with me, but ole boy takes it kind of personal. I guess it was kind of mean, but it was funny. So, I laughed to myself and gave them a sly little wink. You already know I need to add a little gasoline to the fire, so I do my part and play along. I guess I should say, I'm white and they are black, but I'm not a child anymore and I'm over the race shit. I know we are different, but I also know we are the same.

Anyway, when he goes to put a bowl in the microwave again, I whisper as if I don't want "boss" to hear me, and say to him, "Do a good job for him. I don't wanna see boss take you out the house and put you back in the fields." He don't really know if I'm sincere or just talking shit with him. So, he just looks at me. Then, right on queue, one of the other guys say, "You better not burn that shit!" Now he's getting flustered, while the other two are relaxing on the couch (yes, we have a couch, as a matter of fact we have three which is unheard of) and laughing at him. He takes his bowl out of the microwave, and I have no doubt his blood pressure is rising.

I put my bowl back in with the noodles. You see, I put the Mackerel in first, and crisp it up by itself, then I add the noodles, and lastly the pork skins. After this trip to the microwave, I only need one more trip and it's time to eat. I'm not really sure how much more he has to do, but he only makes one more trip after I cook my noodles. As I pour the pork skins are added. I wait for him to come out. They fan the flame once again by telling him, "You need a motherfucking haircut if you're going to work for us." He replies, "I ain't working for y'all, and worry about your own motherfucking hair." He's finally out, and I'm in for my final trip. He is at the table mixing something up when the explosive is thrown into his fire. One guy tells him, "don't be stirring that shit with your pencil Jeffie." He was referencing the goofy-ass puppet my eleven-year-old watches. Apparently, the man knows who "Jeffie" is, so he slams the bowl on the table and walks out without saying a word. They're laughing and telling him to come back, and it seems like the right time, so I start singing "baby come back any kinda of fool can see" just before he makes it to the door.

The three of us share a good laugh before one of the guys on the couch goes to retrieve his friend. It was all good fun, but someone always has to be the butt end of the joke. Today just happened to be his day. I finished my cooking, and it's back on the couch to enjoy it. Just as I finish, the man who sent on the rescue mission returns unsuccessful and the other guys say, "God damnit! Let me get his sensitive ass. I'm hungry." A couple minutes later he returns with his chef in tow, and they are back to business.

That whole scene is just a proof of how it really is most of the time. Don't get me wrong, people get killed, banging kicks off, riots happen, rape happens, as do other things you've heard. So do so many more things that aren't as bad as people may make it out to be. They take us away from everything, but give us us. Sometimes we are all we've got. That's what I want all of you reading this behind these walls to think about. This shit I'm writing is for us, and all of us together can't be stopped. This is our world, just as much as it is anyone else's. I'm tired of being wronged by the ones who represent right. They, in turn, do just as much, if not more, wrong than we do. The only way to stop it is to stick together, black, brown, white and yellow, AB, Ganstas, VL's, Crips, Bloods, Jew, Muslim, and Christian. We are all in this shit together. Who wins if we all fight one another?

Stop doing what they want us to do; read and talk about shit that matters. They want you to watch tv and care more about sports than your current situation. Don't be mad at the man next to you. He is in the same situation as you. When I did my last five years, I fell victim to the bullshit. I lost my smile, learned to hate instead of love, turned potential friends into enemies, because of who they were, which isn't the way. Who is going to fix what is broken if we don't?

That's enough of that for now, plus I'm full and tired. I roll up another roll, walk outside for a smoke, and then crawl in my bunk for bed. As I lay here, I begin to think about the things I'm thankful for, and LIFE of course is at the top of the list. I mean, what else really matters? Without life what would you have? Nothing. Then I think, even the bad times aren't bad, as long as you've got life. Maybe my view of bad and good times is flawed, perhaps they are just life and as long as one still has it, then we should be thankful. Well on second thought, we do experience good and bad times. Either way, we should be thankful for both. Yes, that's the one I'm sticking with, and then I sleep.

The first time my eyes open in paradise is of my own accord, and after being traumatized by fluorescent light and people yelling, "Sleep late, lose weight!" I'm not quite sure how to act. I'm thankful for it, and therefore send a thanks to the boss upstairs. Then I'm on my feet to take a piss, wash my hands, and brush my teeth. After all that it's time for coffee, and get some word in for the day. I tear myself off a rolling paper out of the Holy Book and roll one up. Once outside, I saw the moon and stars for the first time in six months. It was too hectic of a night for me to notice them, but being alone this morning, and the sun has yet to rise, I soak it in. The thumbnail of the moon and morning stars seem a little more beautiful now than ever before. I know it's just me, but I like to think they are shining a little brighter now than ever before.

Once back inside, I glance at the news for about two minutes, which is all I can stomach at one time. I finally greeted the only other person awake at the moment. Then, once again, I wait. Today will be an exciting day. Today is Christmas in prison, also known as canteen day. The pad and pen will finally arrive. I'll also be assigned a job today, and although I'll be whoring myself out for free, working comes with the territory. I hope you didn't think the correction officers were responsible for cooking, cleaning, washing clothes, fixing anything that breaks or otherwise keeping the facility running. We are responsible for all that, and unless you're in a federal facility, you will most likely be doing it all for free. I look at it as modern-day slavery if you're not getting paid for the work you're doing, and as a sweatshop employee if you're working as a federal inmate making $30 - $100 per month. If you don't get paid and a sweatshop employee if they pay you thirty bucks to one hundred and eighty a month in the feds. Apparently minimum wage doesn't apply to us anymore, just like so many constitutional rights they take away from us. I still haven't figured out how you can take rights away from the citizen. Seems like if you did, they would no longer be a citizen, but hey I'm crazy.

Just like that, trays arrive, and I'm sad to say they are no better in this program than they are on the county pretrial side. Fuck my life! But I eat, because I need my strength and then I chill, there was nothing else to do. I worked hard right up until my current incarceration. I needed a little vacation. Certainly, if the choice would've been mine, the location would've been different. I doubt I would stay as long as I'm about to stay here, but I reckon I'll take what I can get.

Then, just as I drifted off for an early morning nap, I was awakened by a cart rolling down the hallway leading to our unit. It's "Penitentiary Santa's Sleigh" making its way towards us with our clear plastic bags full of goodies. The only difference is the guard pushing the cart forgot his red suit and fake beard. We had to purchase our presents at twice the market value, and instead of reindeer there are two convicts covered in jailhouse artwork.

Everyone is up now, proving the point that you can sleep through anything you want, to or be right on time if you wish. You can feel the excitement, and guys are already at the door waiting. I sit up and slide my shower shoes on, I'm not fucking with you when I tell you men are like little children on Christmas morning. Although we know what we ordered, and won't be getting any surprises, we will still be getting something, and of course something is better than nothing. I'm a little better at controlling my emotions than most, but I still enjoy their joy. Don't get me wrong, I'm happy too, but I seem to have a problem with keeping all things in mind.

They call our names, and we walk up to go through our orders to make sure everything we paid for and ordered is there. Then the fun begins. This can also be a dangerous time for those who barter amongst themselves here. Credit is given, and debts must be paid. I sit and observe the hive come alive as men are running to and fro paying debts, collecting debts, and those who are unfortunate enough have no money or support from the outside are trying to get anything the generous will give. It's sad to say but you also have the "extortionist", and "I'll take your shit", type in here who prey on the weak. A lot of times you will have ChoMo's, or child molesters, for those of you who don't know the lingo, paying certain gangs or organizations for protection, which makes no sense to me, but whatever it's their business. Canteen day is a good or bad day depending on your perspective. And just like that, it comes and passes and now I'm ready to write.

Before I get started, I'm called out, assigned a job, and given some tee shirts and another orange uniform. I'll be working on police cars and anything else that breaks down here at the jail. I could've figured this, as I'm an infamous criminal around here, but at the same time, was a business owner, all around handy guy, and some might even dare go as far as saying a "good guy." Being a mixture of all that sometimes confuses me, but whatever, I am what I am.

After assignment and wardrobe pickup, I'm back in the unit, because it's Friday and I won't start work until Monday. The only other thing I've got going this weekend is a visit tomorrow, that I'm highly looking forward to, as it will be the first time in six months, I'll be able to hug my loved ones. Actually, the first time I'll be able to physically lay my eyes on my boys. They are both children and haven't been allowed to visit until now. In a perfect world that would be cruel and unusual punishment, but the world is far from perfect and for some reason no one seems to give a fuck about anything unless it directly impacts them. That's one for humanity right there and zero for the good Lord.

Maybe I should start the book off with that line? Now that

I'm back in the unit, at the table with pen in hand, I'm not quite sure what I can write to open eyes, do some good, and say what needs to be said, all the while not losing my life in the process. Dr. King told his thoughts and dreams in a nonfiction way, and we all know what that got him. Therefore, "this is a fictional story I've just told you," will be the beginning, the middle, and the end for me. You decide if it's true, or if I'm just crazy.

10 The End of the Matter

What more can I say? A lot of course. If you don't have it by now, I'm not sure if I can give it to you. I hit on all the points I thought most prison books leave out. For some reason people only want to talk about bad shit that happens ten percent of the time and never the rest of the story. Hopefully, you now know what it's like to walk in another man's shoes, and hopefully this book sparks the same thing in all of you that is burning inside of me. It is up to us!

120

9 781960 853332